The Battle of Hillsboro

eXtremely Offensive
15TH Anniversary Edition

Jesse S. Smith

BASEMENTIA PUBLICATIONS
SILVERTON, OR

THE BATTLE OF HILLSBORO: EXTREMELY OFFENSIVE 15TH ANNIVERSARY EDITION

Copyright ©2009, ©2024 by Jesse S. Smith

Published by Basementia Publications
Silverton, OR

15th Anniversary Edition April 2024
First edition first printing December 2009

Paperback ISBN 978-1-958337-12-7
Hardcover ISBN 978-1-958337-13-4

None of the elements of this story should be mistaken for real people, real places, real events, or good ideas. They are not.

Cover photo by @dlewis33 via iStock ©2008

Fiction / Satire / Transgressive / Noir Thriller / Heist Caper / Crime Spree

Preface to the 15th Anniversary Edition

It has been 15 years since I first published *The Battle of Hillsboro*, and the story is still relevant today.

Although tobacco smoking is no longer allowed in bars; and Western media is no longer dominated by daily headlines about terrorist tactics: the larger themes and attitudes discussed herein are as current as ever, and perhaps more so.

Today, all around me, not only on social media and at formal political meetings, but even in my personal life: in their "jokes," in their offhand remarks, and even in their well-thought-out arguments, sometimes subtly and sometimes in shockingly blunt terms, people who *really* should know better seem to have a sort of sick fascination with the self-destructive idea of a violent uprising against our cherished principles of democracy.

The characters in *The Battle of Hillsboro* felt exactly the same way: and that's precisely why this book is more relevant than ever today.

When I wrote it, *The Battle of Hillsboro* was a thinly disguised metaphor for the 2003 US-led invasion of Iraq.

Today, almost without changing a damn thing, the same book is a thinly disguised metaphor for the horrific potential consequences of the Marxist-Anarchist agitprop (or its Christian Nationalist counterpart) which especially since 2018 has become such a notable feature of our culture.

The moral of *The Battle of Hillsboro* remains the same: **War is bad.**

I have corrected a few typos, smoothed some sentences; inserted one or two incendiary remarks, well, maybe three or four incendiary remarks, okay I didn't count the incendiary remarks but I'm sure I added a few; ahem, and I amended the fictional group's official recruitment policies. Otherwise, this is the same raw and riveting crime spree action-adventure that I had a blast writing and many of my friends enjoyed reading, 15 or more years ago.

The original version owed a huge thanks to Tony Martinelli for suggesting several very reasonable edits; to Owen Meyer for pointing out a glaring factual error in the first printing; and of course to Jon Rigby and Andy Hoke for reviewing my early drafts and offering their thoughts. Thank you all. (Don't blame these dudes for the changes I have made in this latest version, it's not their fault.)

I originally drafted most of *The Battle of Hillsboro* in 2007. What with all the revisions and edits and whatnot, the first printing was released in 2009.

Yes, this book first came out in 2009, folks. I can hardly believe it has already been 15 years since then. I am no longer as young as I once was... although ironically, I might be in better shape now than I was back then.

I have written and released several other books in the meantime, but *The Battle of Hillsboro* remains my most popular work of fiction to date. It's easy to understand why. The book is short, it's action-packed, and it's offensive. There's sex and drugs and violence. What's not to like?

Just be aware, before you turn the next page, that this is the "**eXtremely Offensive 15th Anniversary Edition**."

If you're the sort of person who's easily offended, then this is **not** the book for you.

Suck my dick, motherfuckers! Have a great day.

-JJ

Chapter 1

It was just another evening out at the bar with the guys until we decided to start a war.

The music was too loud. A neon sign advertising overpriced piss beer glowed in the window. The sour bartender in her "MEN SUCK" t-shirt kept me waiting for a long time while she chatted with some other patrons at the far end of the bar. At length, she stood before me and wordlessly eyed my flannel shirt and stubbly masculine chin. I smiled, and asked for a pitcher. She poured the beer with an air of resentful, dismissive hostility, and rather pointedly said nothing to me other than the price. I tipped her anyway, and wondered why, as I brought the pitcher back to the table.

We were taking turns buying rounds, and soon the four of us would have consumed a whole pitcher each. Even drinking cheap swill, I was feeling more than a little tipsy.

"I'm just so fucking sick of it," Drew was saying, puffing desperately on his cigarette, as though some disaster was imminent unless he could suck the whole thing down in a matter of moments.

"The game is decided before you start," agreed Victor. "You need all these *things* to win, but you can't get the things unless you've already won."

"Like what?" I asked, topping off everyone's glasses.

"Take housing, for example," said Johnny. "If you want to rent an apartment, you have to be able to plunk down a huge chunk of cash just to move in, *and* you need to be able to prove that you're employed, and usually you have to have a rental history. But in order to be employed, you have to have a house where you can take a shower, you have to own some decent clothes, and you have to have an address and phone number to put on your job application where potential employers can get back to you. If you don't have a place to live, you can't get a job; and if you don't have a job, you can't get a place to live. Catch-22."

"So Johnny," said Victor.

"Yes?"

"You have a place to live."

"Uh-huh…"

"Then why don't you ever take a shower?"

We all laughed at that, but when the guffaws died down it was apparent that Drew was still brooding. Drew was employed, as it happened; but his job was a dead end, and did not pay well.

"There's got to be another way," I said sympathetically, "instead of working your whole life for The Man and getting paid dick."

"You still want to conquer the world," said Victor to me derisively.

"I'll drink to that," I said.

"How are you going to do it?" he pressed, a trifle belligerently.

"Well," I said awkwardly, looking down at the table, "I had this great plan to become rich and famous, but…" I paused, with more words in my head than I could get out of my mouth. I decided this was not the time to enumerate my many failures. "It hasn't worked out yet," I summarized.

"Yeah," said Drew, lighting a new cigarette from the glowing butt of the one he had just finished, "it's a tough world to conquer."

"You could take it by force," suggested Johnny.

Normally we would have laughed and changed the subject. Normally we would have finished our beers, gotten high in the parking lot, and gone our separate ways. But these are trying times, and there was something strange in Johnny's voice, something that resonated with each of us. Nobody laughed. There was a pause.

"It's been tried," said Victor skeptically. "It never works."

"The Roman Empire lasted for centuries," I posited.

"That wasn't the whole world," objected Drew.

"I'd settle for the Roman Empire," I said. "I don't need the whole world. Just a big fat chunk of it."

"But the Roman Empire collapsed in the end," Victor protested.

"Everything comes to an end eventually," said Johnny philosophically. "Eventually the Earth will crash into the Sun and that will be the end of all this."

"You guys are smoking crack," said Victor.

"Still, it's an interesting idea," I said, "on a strictly hypothetical basis."

"Hypothetically, of course," agreed Drew.

"So Johnny," I asked. "What would it take to raise an army that could conquer a new Roman Empire?"

Drew answered first. "You don't have to raise an army that big," he opined. "All you have to do is take control of the existing American military. If you could do that, you'd have all the firepower you'd need."

I doubted that, but Johnny voiced my doubts for me. "No," he said, "you'd need more manpower, if you really wanted to conquer the world. I don't even know what it would take. I'm guessing maybe 20 million soldiers, at least, and a huge navy and air force."

"Wait, are we conquering the whole world, or just Rome?" asked Drew.

"Both," I said.

"Neither," said Johnny.

"You guys couldn't conquer a flower pot," said Victor.

"I conquered your Mom," replied Drew.

"The question," Johnny continued unperturbed, "is how we would take control of the US military. I doubt any of us could get elected to the Presidency. And if we overthrew the government, the military would try to oust us; they would not accept our leadership."

"So we have to start smaller," I said.

I might be anyone. You don't know me. You wouldn't recognize me if you saw me. I might just look like some grungy jerkoff who spends too much time drinking beer and sitting in front of a computer: greasy, unshaven, somewhat pudgy, with dark circles under his puffy red eyes, and food stains on his rumpled, faded, ratty old T-shirt. Then again, I might not look like that at all. In fact, despite what you may think, the big secret is that in reality I look a lot like a certain movie star: suave, confident, muscular, and stylishly dressed. Really, I do. Yeah, I have to work out for hours every day to maintain this physique. All that time at the gym really cuts into my social life, but it's worth it. I'm telling you: it's worth it because the ladies dig me. They sure do. (Maybe not the bartender here; but *other* ladies.) When they see me, the ladies are like, "Masculinity is toxic, and men are pigs, but ooh, you have such... big... muscles..." And they move in real close to me, and then their breath gets all heavy, and their eyes kinda glaze over, and they start making these little sighs and moaning noises, and next thing I know I find myself saying things like, "Who are you? Are you aware that we're in a restaurant? Is that your husband over there? Put your shirt back on, lady!" Actually come to think of it, being this good-looking can be pretty awkward sometimes; but it's who I've decided to be, so I've just got to live with the downsides, such as they are: and if that means random women swarm all over me everywhere I go, then so be it. Somehow, I will survive.

"We have to start smaller," Johnny indicated his agreement by echoing my brief summary of our takeover strategy thus far. "We can't just nab hold of the US government without anybody noticing. So instead, basically, we take control of a tribal area, we hold it, and then we can spread our power and sphere of influence more gradually as we expand our empire."

Johnny was an unlikely individual to be delivering such a speech. He was tall but quite slender, with long dark hair in a pony tail, and a wisp of moustache and minimalist goatee. He had a tendency to dress all in black, and to listen to a lot of psy-trance and Nine Inch Nails.

"Wouldn't you still need an army?" asked Drew. "How would you control a tribal area unless you had an army? And do you mean a tribal area in Pakistan, or what?"

Drew was a giant of a man, and built like a pro wrestler; not because he exercised, but just because that was the way he was built.

"No, no, a tribal area right here," explained Johnny. "You can always raise an army if you have enough money; and you can always get more money if you're not afraid to use your army."

"It's like a reverse Catch-22," said Victor admiringly.

You don't know Victor either. He could be anyone. Don't imagine him as an adult version of a little kid who likes video games and sci-fi TV; he doesn't look like that at all. No, Victor looks like Al Pacino in *The Godfather*, if the Corleones were prone to wearing black leather biker jackets.

"But where would we get the money to start with?" Drew asked. "None of us have any."

"You go around causing havoc and mayhem," answered Johnny, our military strategist. "Pretty soon you'll have more money than you know what to do with."

"Here's to havoc and mayhem!" I said, raising my glass.

We toasted to havoc, mayhem, chaos, anarchy and empire-building. Then we got high in the parking lot and went our separate ways.

But by then it was too late. Though we had carefully coached the conversation in hypothetical terms, we all knew each other too well to be fooled by the premise. The thought of causing massive destruction was a rush. The idea of power, real power, huge widespread power backed by deadly force: this idea was a serious turn-on, a sinister thing so fascinating that once glimpsed our eyes could not turn away from it, as though the idea were some scaly winged Gorgon and we mortals had been turned to stone at the sight of it and were now doomed to stare towards it for the rest of eternity without blinking.

Chapter 2

We each tried not to think about it. We each grappled with the impossibility of accepting the lives we had and making the best of them. And we each independently came to the realization that trying to live normal lives would eventually kill us, just as surely as the police would kill us if we implemented our crazy idea.

We decided to brave the police.

I had not seen or communicated with any of the other guys for a week since our night at the bar. I was home alone, sharpening knives. I was seated on the floor with more than a dozen knives surrounding me in a semicircle, and I sharpened them while I watched TV. There were kitchen knives, steak knives, a butcher knife, even a butter knife which I had painstakingly sharpened to a deadly point. Having conducted this operation once, I decided it was a total waste of time and elected not to go through the same procedure again. My favorite though was a cheap butterfly knife I had purchased at a convenience store. Next to the knives was my old baseball bat on one side, and on the other side were some common household cleaning products which, I had heard, could be quite deadly when combined. I had resisted the urge to use the Internet to research the steps necessary to make explosives, because I did not want the FBI to show up at my door.

The phone rang. It was Victor.

"Hey dude," I said.

"Hey," he said. "How goes conquering the world?"

"I'm working on it," I said, as I picked my knife back up and kept sharpening.

"Yeah," he said, "right on. Tell you what man, want to grab a beer?"

"Sure thing."

Victor was already at the bar when I arrived.

"I can't stop thinking about it," he told me.

"About what?" I asked, even though I already knew.

"Chaos," he said. "Mayhem. And the idea of seizing power like an old feudal baron or something. It's ridiculous, suicidal, totally stupid, and yet…"

"Have you talked to the other guys about it?" I asked.

"Well, I called Johnny yesterday, just got his voicemail, haven't heard back."

"Don't take it personally," I told him.

"I know," he said. "Johnny's not much of a phone person."

"So what have you done about it?" I asked. "Made any plans?"

"A few," he said, "but they all require a team. But you know what I did do." Before elucidating his actions, he looked around to make sure nobody was looking in our direction. Then he leaned forward conspiratorially, and opened his jacket enough to reveal the handle of a pistol.

"Where did you get that?" I asked admiringly.

"I stole it," he told me. "It used to be my Dad's. I don't think my Mom even knew it was there; so she won't miss it."

"Well don't let anybody see you with it," I said in a voice low enough that it would be covered by the music. It was really awful music, some asshole had put a goddamn country song on the juke box and I wondered, not for the first time, why we always came to this shitty bar anyway. "I think you need a permit to carry a concealed-"

"Listen to you, talking about permits and shit. Some fucking anarchist you are."

"I'm just paranoid," I replied; and this was true.

"So, okay, Mr. Paranoid, what about you? Have you been thinking about all this?"

I nodded.

"And?"

"Knives," I told him. "Lots of knives. And chemicals to make mustard gas."

"Mustard gas?" he repeated, far too loudly for my sensitivities. "Man, you don't fuck around, violating the Geneva Conventions with chemical weapons and shit."

"It's not very practical," I admitted, "because I don't have a gas mask. Not to mention, it would be better if we could seize power without killing a whole bunch of civilians." I tried to keep my voice low. Nobody seemed to care what we were talking about anyway.

"Yeah," Victor said distractedly. "Listen. Do you think the other guys are on board with this?"

"I don't know, man, we'll have to ask them. Maybe. I mean, they were interested, when we discussed it before, but I don't know if that necessarily means they'd be willing to follow through."

"Right," said Victor, clearly thinking so hard he looked like he was going to give himself an aneurysm.

"Why don't we ask them?" I suggested.

"Well, if they're not into it, they could rat us out to the police before we even got started."

"And I thought I was the paranoid one. No, dude, they wouldn't do that."

"How can you be sure?" he asked.

"They're our friends!" I answered. "Besides, it was pretty much their idea."

"It just bothers me that Johnny hasn't called me back."

"Don't let it get to you. Johnny will turn up eventually. What about Drew? Have you talked to him yet?"

"No," he said flatly. I waited for an explanation but none was forthcoming.

"Well, let's call him," I suggested brightly, and whipped out my cell phone.

"I don't know if he would be much help," Victor pouted.

"We're talking about raising an army, right?" I pointed out. "I think we're going to need all the help we can get."

Victor seemed inclined to argue, I wasn't sure why, and I didn't particularly care. I was just looking up Drew's number in my phone when he walked in the door of the bar.

"Hey wassup brothers!" he called out when he saw us.

"Dude! I was just about to call you," I told him, waving my cell phone as evidence.

"Well," he replied, "here I am!"

Victor acknowledged Drew, a bit distantly I thought. Drew went up to the bar to see about distracting the bartender from her personal conversation long enough to serve him a drink.

I considered asking Victor what he had against Drew, but it didn't really matter to me, so instead I suggested that we should try again to get Johnny to come out of his hole.

"I'm telling you," said Victor, "he's not answering his phone."

"With Johnny, you have to catch him at the right time," I suggested. "If you call when he's working on something, you'll never get him, so you have to get him right at precisely the moment when he's taking a break or whatever."

Victor looked unconvinced but I dialed Johnny's number. He picked up after the fourth ring.

"Hey, Johnny!" I said, giving Victor a thumbs-up. "We're all over here at the bar and we think you should join us."

"I don't know, man," Johnny answered dryly, "I'm working on something."

"Take a break, dude. You could use it. Let your brain sort out your problems in the background for a while."

There was a pause, and then Johnny replied wearily, "All right, but I can't stay out too late tonight. I have things to do tomorrow."

"Sure thing buddy," I told him. "I'm sure we all feel the same way."

Naturally, we were up until the sun rose. When they kicked us out of the bar we all went back to Johnny's apartment and lounged in his living room planning our war.

Johnny went off on a long tangential discourse, during which he explained to us all that "Control, in this context, would refer specifically to civic control, militarily enforced by our legions. I mean, look at the drug cartels in Mexico. Every one of them employs a private army, and together they're more powerful than the government."

This is nuts, I was thinking. *There's no way we'll get enough people to follow us.*

"Dude, are you seriously suggesting that the four of us could take and hold a town of 30,000 people?" I asked. I didn't even know how many people would live in the town; I just pulled a number out of the air.

"Well, not by ourselves," he replied seriously, "and not for several months. We'll have to make some preparations."

Initially, we discussed invading the nearby town of Hillsboro. It was a small town, or rather, that was our impression of it; and it was remote, or rather, we had always thought of it as fairly remote. However, when we gave the matter a little more thought, after some time with several online data sources, we concluded that Hillsboro itself was actually too large for our purposes. Hillsboro had its own airport; it had a population too large for a small militia to easily control; it had lots of small streets leading in and out, which would make a blockade nearly impossible; and finally, when we thought about it a little more, Hillsboro was simply too close to other urban centers.

Hillsboro was not a viable target.

So we selected a target that was more appropriately suited to our mission: someplace large enough to have several banks and a shopping district but small enough that we would be able to launch a meaningful assault; someplace with limited road accessibility, so we would have to man as few barricades as possible; and most importantly, someplace far enough out in the middle of nowhere that the Sheriff's department would be minimally staffed and it would be several hours, if not a day or more, before the National Guard would be able to mount an effective response. Our strategy depended on carrying out our assault quickly, then consolidating our power to retain our gains. If the Sheriff or National Guard were able to respond quickly, they could prevent us from fortifying our positions and all would be lost.

"So check out this map," Johnny said, and we all crowded around his computer, where he had pulled up satellite imagery overlaid with a roadmap. "Look, here, this is a small town out in the middle of nowhere," he zoomed out and pointed for a sense of location, then zoomed back in, "with only two main arterials leading in and out. Two-man teams could hold those for quite a while against militarily superior forces."

And with that, we chose a target town that was not Hillsboro; but still, whenever we made reference to our upcoming operation, we always called it the Battle of Hillsboro. The name stuck. It was catchy somehow, the way a tune gets stuck in your head, perhaps because the phrase seemed like such a non sequitur, Hillsboro being such a tranquil, placid, even boring place, where no battle had ever been fought. Also, by referring to a non-target as though it were a target, we hoped to confuse any would-be informants, should any of our junior recruits prove to be spies and infiltrators, which was always a possibility.

Our plan was beginning to take shape.

Chapter 3

It was dark. A few blocks away I could hear a few raucous revelers whooping. A police squad car cruised slowly past, but they did not see Victor and me, crouched in our hiding place behind a dumpster in an alley.

We had staked out a spot where two or three suitable cars were parked. I just hoped that when their owners arrived, they would be alone. I wanted this to be as simple as possible.

The waiting was killing me. My legs were cramped from crouching too long. I was cold, nervous, and far too sober to be getting myself into such a stupid situation. Doubts and second thoughts crossed and re-crossed my mind, as I reminded myself once again that everything about Johnny's plan was stupid and suicidal. *What if the owners of these cars already went home with other people?* I wondered. *We might be crouched in this alley all night.* I hoped some drunken fool wouldn't mistake our hiding place for a good place to take a piss; but from the smell of the place, if someone did, he wouldn't be the first.

Suddenly my reverie was interrupted as a young man walked up to one of the cars we were watching. He appeared to be alone, slightly unsteady, but due to our inattentiveness he was nearly in the car already. We couldn't let him escape.

I looked at Victor. We nodded at each other behind the T-shirts we had tied over our faces, and bolted out into the street. The guy already had one foot in the car but it was too late, we were on him. I grabbed his shoulder and pulled him out of the car.

Though startled, he recovered quickly, and was just making a move as though he was preparing to try to punch me when he heard the click of Victor's pistol being cocked in his ear.

"Don't make any noise and you won't get hurt," said Victor. The guy nodded and went limp. I pulled him back into the alley, where we went through his pockets, took his keys and his cell phone and his pathetic three dollars in cash. We didn't even want his maxed-out credit cards. We tied him up with duct tape and gagged him, and left him in a dumpster in the alley. We hoped this would give us an hour before the vehicle was reported stolen.

Having chucked the guy into a dumpster all wrapped in duct tape, we got into his car, an old Subaru station wagon. I drove us to the rendezvous point, where we met up with Johnny and Drew. They were sporting a brand-new monster pickup truck, complete with canopy: one of those rigs that are half speed racer, half tank, nearly as large as a semi. It was the kind of truck that costs a small fortune and is always shiny and new because they are purely a status symbol and used solely for single passenger commuting in town: never for any actual farm work.

"Ain't she a beaut?" said Johnny proudly, patting the vehicle with affection.

"Very nice," I said. I couldn't believe I was involved in all this. It didn't seem real; it felt more like I was a character in a video game.

"Where's the gun store?" asked Victor.

Johnny pointed. "Just down the road, that way, on the southwest corner. The building is constructed of concrete cinder blocks, it is a fucking fortress. There are windows on either side of the front door, and the front door itself has a window in it, too; but all the windows are reinforced with heavy steel bars."

"You crazy bitches," said Drew, dropping and stepping on his cigarette.

"I think I have it figured out," said Johnny casually, ignoring Drew's outburst.

He explained, and we each took our places according to Johnny's plan.

I climbed into the back of the truck and found there a heavy-duty chain that ended in a sturdy hook. Victor drove the station wagon around the corner from the store's front entrance and stayed parked at the curb, engine running, lights out, in gear, using the e-brake to keep it from rolling so the brake lights wouldn't light up. Drew walked to the door of the store and waited in the shadows as Johnny got in the truck and drove it right up in front of the store. He hadn't even come to a stop before I jumped out the back with the chain. I don't know where he got that chain from; it was rusty like it had been sitting out in the rain for a long time, but the metal in the links was so thick that I thought it could hold the anchor for a giant ocean freighter. Drew passed the chain under the steel grill that protected the door and hooked it back over on itself while I attached the other end to the back of the truck, using not just the trailer hitch but the frame of the pickup as well. In seconds we gave Johnny the thumbs-up, and he accelerated the pickup as fast as he could; but when the chain had reached its full length and pulled taut, the truck slowed down instead of pulling the grid out of the wall. The steel bars were fastened solidly, with heavy bolts deep into the door. I wondered if this plan was really going to work. Johnny stopped the truck, reversed back until the rear wheels were up on the curb, put the truck in neutral while he revved up the engine, and then put it in gear. The truck jumped forward, its wheels squealing, acrid blue smoke coming off its tires. This time when the chain reached its full length, the bottom part of the steel grid popped out; but the rest remained securely bolted to the door. The chain came unfastened from the grid and skittered behind the truck. Johnny stopped the truck and stuck his head out the window to survey the scene. Then he drove off down the street.

"Where the fuck is he going?" shouted Drew.

Johnny was already executing a wide U-turn in the middle of the street. He revved the engine, a block and a half away, and I knew what he was going to do.

"Shit," I said, "get the fuck out of his way." I tugged at Drew's sleeve and ran. I could hear Drew behind me as the truck accelerated, going faster and faster as it got closer and closer until with a catastrophic crunching sound it plowed right into the front of the building. The engine died, grinding painfully. The air bags deployed. Inside the building, a security alarm was ringing.

"Johnny," I said, running back to the truck, "holy shit dude, are you all right?"

Looking somewhat shaken, Johnny nodded and motioned us inside the store. We had to climb over the hood of the truck and kick bits of the door out of the way, but this was easily accomplished, and then there we were.

"See if there's a back door," I suggested to Drew over the clang of the alarm, and then I set to work surveying the merchandise. I quickly made a pile of hunting rifles, shotguns, and ammunition. I tried to smash a glass case to get at the hunting knives and high powered scopes, but either I was too nervous or else the shatter-resistant plexiglass was too strong.

Then Johnny was beside me with a pair of bolt cutters and a large duffel bag, the army surplus variety. Drew returned, saying he had managed to unlock and open the steel door in the rear of the building. Then he and I set to work filling the duffel bag while Johnny used the bolt cutters to open various cases. He came up with an armload of handguns, which was almost more than we could stuff into the duffel bag. I wanted to break into the case with the scopes and knives, too, but

Johnny screamed over the clamor of the alarm system, "There's no time! Come on! Let's get the fuck out of here!"

Drew grabbed the duffel and casually slung it over his shoulder, even though the thing must have weighed 80 pounds with all the bullets and guns we had stuffed in there. Johnny limped after him, and I reluctantly followed, feeling I was forgetting something. As we neared the back exit of the store I saw it: a gas mask with protective goggles, and across the aisle, a whole rack of Kevlar vests. I loaded my arms and hurried after my friends.

We were stuffing this booty into the hatchback of the stolen Subaru when a car pulled up. Some dumbass thought he was going to be a Good Samaritan.

"Oh my God," he called out through his open window. He was looking at the truck that had smashed into the front of the building. Its engine was smoking. "Is everyone all right?"

We looked at each other, then at him. Couldn't he see that we were wearing black masks over our faces? Did he think we were with the Boy Scouts? Perhaps he was mentally defective.

Suddenly Victor sprang out from behind the wheel. In two paces he had reached the interloper's vehicle. He flung the door open and stuck his gun in the guy's face.

"Get out of the fucking car!" he said.

"But, what-" protested the frightened man.

"I said get the fuck out!" yelled Victor. When the man did not move, I reached through the window with my butterfly knife. As the guy finally registered fear I cut through his seat belt, opened the door, and hauled him out of the car by the front of his shirt. The Good Samaritan's car was still in drive, and without his foot on the brake, it began rolling across the intersection, until it eventually came to rest against a stop sign on the far side. We pushed the frightened man inside the gun shop and closed the back door on him. That would confuse the police.

Then we all piled into the station wagon and drove off; not a minute too soon, for as we were driving away from the scene, a police car pulled up in front of the store, its lights flashing in the dark night. A block later, a second police car passed us, heading in the other direction, towards the store we had just robbed.

Never in my life had I experienced such an adrenaline rush.

We drove the stolen Subaru back to where Johnny's own pickup truck was parked, a much smaller, older, and more beat-up truck than the one he had just destroyed. We unloaded the gear from the station wagon and flung it into the back of Johnny's truck; then the others all piled into the truck while I ditched the Subaru. I was so scared I was shaking, imagining that at any moment I would be apprehended by the police, driving a stolen vehicle that had been used as an accessory to an armed robbery. I left the car in some residential district, and I dropped the keys down a sewer grate a block away. Then I walked back to my own car, trying to look normal, as normal as a guy can look at four in the morning walking down a dark street trying to disentangle himself from the T-shirt that had been tied around his head.

"I need to get a fucking ski mask," I muttered to myself while stuffing the T-shirt and my used latex gloves into random trash cans as I passed by.

I found my own car and with my hands shaking managed to get the door open and drive to Johnny's place. The other two guys had already bailed. Johnny was waiting for me next to his truck. Saying very little, we transferred my share of the stolen firearms and gear from his vehicle to mine. Then we were done and I was ready to go home. I held out my hand, and he shook it.

"Nice work," I said.

"You too," he replied. There was a pause, during which I suddenly realized how tired I was. I wanted to ask if he thought we would really get away with it. I wanted to ask if he still wanted to go through with the rest of the plan. But words failed me, and instead I just nodded my head and said, "See you later."

"See you," he said, and nodded back.

Chapter 4

I thought I was paranoid before; but that wasn't anything compared to what I was feeling now. What if one of my neighbors had seen me unloading my new stash of firearms in the middle of the night and reported me to the police? What if some hidden video surveillance camera had caught me donning my T-shirt mask and stealing that car at gunpoint with Victor? The fact that I had not held the gun would not command much leniency at my sentencing hearing. We had worn gloves and masks throughout the operation, but what if we missed some crucial detail? I was sure there were a frighteningly large number of high-tech techniques the law might be able to use to identify me. Maybe they would be able to distinguish me by the clothes I had been wearing. Maybe they would find a single strand of my hair somewhere in the stolen car, or at the gun store, and they could track me down with some top secret DNA database. In a fit of paranoia, I shaved my head, feeling like the guy in the movie of Pink Floyd's *The Wall*. I was sure my phone was tapped. I was certain someone was snooping through my e-mails. Maybe the police were on their way up to my apartment right now. Maybe they were standing outside the door, this very moment, a whole heavily armed SWAT team about to burst in. What was that? Did you hear something?

I disconnected my phone. I unplugged my computer. I started drinking too much; it was the only way I could get to sleep at night. Every morning I showed up at work late, hung over and sleep deprived. After a week I stopped offering excuses. After another week they fired me. This was a relief, because braving cross-town traffic every morning had become more than my nerves could handle. I went into total panic mode every time I saw a traffic cop, and had to restrain myself from pulling some ridiculous stunt that would result in a car chase like you see on those goddamn TV shows. Getting fired solved some of my problems temporarily; at least now I only had to leave the house to buy booze and fast food.

Needless to say I felt like total shit by the time my friends tracked me down. I didn't know what day of the week it was. I was watching TV late at night with all the lights off and the volume low when I was sure I heard the floorboards creak outside my door. I took a sloppy swig of cheap booze straight from the bottle and pulled one of my stolen handguns out from under the couch cushions. I chambered a round and turned the safety off. I pointed the gun at the door.

Someone knocked. It startled me so much I almost convulsively pulled the trigger. After a moment, when I still hadn't said anything, there was another knock.

"Who is it?" I managed, fighting to keep the panic out of my voice.

"Hey dude, it's Drew," came the welcome sound of my friend's voice, and a flood of relief surged through me, followed by a second wave of fear: maybe the cops had him at gunpoint and were just using him to get me to open my door without a fight. I kept the gun aimed at the door.

"Are you alone?" I asked.

"Except for these two hookers I brought with me," came the reply. "Yeah I'm alone. Come on man, open up."

Although I looked through it, I didn't trust the door's peephole; too easy for someone to stand off to the side. I kept the chain secured, painfully aware of its flimsiness; a good solid kick from the outside would pop that chain right out of the door frame, much more easily than the bars had come out of the gun shop door. I stood with my body blocking the door, to try to prevent such an attack, and opened it a crack.

There was Drew, smiling, some kind of zippered carryall in one hand. No police or other coercive entity was in evidence.

"It's just me, man," he said.

I had to pause to collect my thoughts. Finally I said, "All right. Just a second." I closed the door, slid the chain out of its catch, and then opened the door halfway. Drew had to turn sideways, but he came in. I closed the door immediately behind him, threw the deadbolt to, and replaced the chain.

"Are you all right, man?" he asked.

"Yeah," I said, my head reeling. "I'm fine. I just need to sit down." I flopped on the couch, put the safety on the gun, and haphazardly tossed it onto the coffee table, where it was lost amid a pile of pizza boxes, fast food wrappers, dirty dishes, and empty bottles.

"Dude," he said, looking around, "you need to get out more."

I didn't feel like taking advice from him or anyone, so I made no reply.

"Can we at least open a window in here?" he asked. I begrudgingly nodded my head. As he was opening the window I reached for my bottle of rotgut liquor.

"Whoah," he said, "there's your problem. Hey. Don't drink no more of that cheap shit. Looky here." With that he opened his zippered bag, rifled through its contents, and retrieved a bottle of top-shelf bourbon. "Have some of this," he explained, lighting a cigarette. "It will fix you right up."

I was quite surprised to discover how right he was. Two hours later the bottle of bourbon was empty, I was bumming smokes off Drew, watching the room spin drunkenly around me. We were laughing and laughing about nothing at all, egging each other on with stupid jokes. It was the best I had felt in weeks; the best I had felt, in fact, since before the gun store robbery.

Finally I felt drunk enough to ask Drew about what was on my mind

"Hey man," I said, now in something approaching a whisper, "do you think they'll figure out it was us?"

"Nah," he said dismissively. "We were careful. No fingerprints; faces covered; and the getaway car was stolen. The surveillance tapes won't tell them a damn thing. There's nothing they can use to connect it back to us."

"God damn, I hope you're right," I said, peeping out the corner of my blinds at the street below to see if there was anyone staking us out.

"Relax, dude," he said. "Of course I'm right. The whole operation went according to plan, and now we've been laying low for a month. If they knew it was us, they would have come for us by now."

"Has it been a month?" I asked, my eyes wide with surprise. I sloshed some of the cheap booze into my glass; the good stuff was all gone, and I wasn't ready to stop drinking. "I had no idea it had been that long."

"I told you, you need to get out, man. You're afraid of getting found, but you're more likely to draw attention to yourself, living like this and shaving your head. You got to pull it together."

"Yeah," I said morosely. My life had fallen apart. I could hardly believe it, but if Drew was right, I had neither checked my e-mail nor talked on the phone for weeks. What surprised me the most was that I didn't miss it at all. I wondered if I had missed even one single important message in all that time, and I doubted it. I didn't even care who might have been trying to call me or IM me. I didn't want to talk to anyone anyway.

But there was a more important crisis brewing in the immediate present, a crisis of critical proportions.

"We're almost out of booze," I said, holding up my bottle of rotgut liquor to show Drew the few remaining drops at the bottom. He wrinkled his nose in distaste at my choice of beverages and responded, "Yeah, and I'm about out of smokes, too."

"What should we do?" I asked. I figured either Drew would go home or else he would volunteer to drive to the store. Instead he reached back into his little zippered bag and began pulling out various implements. It took a moment before I registered what they were: ski masks, a box of latex gloves, and a .45 semiautomatic.

"Right now?" I asked.

"No time like the present," he said, stuffing the gun into his belt and pulling on a pair of gloves.

"But I'm so drunk," I protested vaguely.

"I'll do the talking," he offered; and even though I was certain that he was just as drunk as I was, this was somehow comforting to me.

"Some fucking empire-building," I commented savagely. "We're just a couple of thugs robbing a convenience store."

"Everybody's got to start somewhere," he said.

Chapter 5

We burst through the automatic sliding doors with masks on and guns drawn.

"Get down on the fucking floor," Drew said to the people in line at the counter.

"Keep your hands where I can see them," I told the cashier, who had obviously been reaching for his little hidden button to call the police. He raised his hands into the air.

"I said get the fuck down!" Drew was screaming at a large customer, some hick who looked like an ex-football player and who clearly thought that he could take us. The guy did not listen. He had nearly walked close enough to grab Drew's gun. I couldn't let it end like this. I took my gun off the cashier long enough to shoot the hick in the leg. Tough though he was, he crumpled to the floor and began moaning. I was amazed that I'd been able to hit him at all. I turned my gun back to the cashier. "Just follow instructions and nobody, um, nobody else gets hurt," I said. The cashier nodded wordlessly. That poor fuck was getting paid minimum wage, I supposed, and he had to work the late shift; surely not enough compensation for having a gun stuck in his face.

"Open up the till," I instructed. As the cashier obeyed my order I thought, *Wasn't Drew going to do all the talking?* But he had his hands full: he was trying to do crowd control and simultaneously load up a bag with as much beer and wine as would fit. The bag was an old travel bag we found in my closet. We had carefully removed or obliterated all airline tags and ownership markings. "Now, get down on the floor with them," I told the clerk. He moved around the counter and laid belly down on the floor. I took all the cash out of the till; then I lifted up the tray and took the larger bills from underneath. Everyone knows the night clerk doesn't have the keys or codes to the safe; there was no time to waste fucking with that. I stuffed the money into a pillowcase I had brought along; then I grabbed all the cartons the store had in stock of Drew's favorite brand of cigarettes. Drew reappeared at that moment, and said "Let's go, man." I nodded. We backed out the store's automatic sliding doors, keeping our guns on the prone patrons on the floor. Then we took off running.

Drew's travel bag full of bottles made a clattering, clanging, clamorous cacophony like a klaxon as we high-tailed it down the street wearing our ski masks, each of us carrying a gun and a bag full of stolen property. It was far too obvious that we had just conducted an armed robbery. People driving by in cars were honking, staring at us. I brandished my weapon at one, and they kept driving; but I was certain that someone must have called the cops by now. We had to get off the street. We couldn't drive off in a getaway vehicle because we hadn't brought one; the convenience store was just three blocks from my abode. We couldn't go straight back there, either, because we would be sure to be followed, tracked down and hunted.

I began to realize that this adventure was not as well-planned as our previous heist. I was no longer certain that we would get away with it; and that thought was very frightening.

This was not the time for regrets or second thoughts. I tried to focus on keeping my drunken ass running, putting one foot in front of the other. Intoxicated and out of shape, I knew I couldn't keep this up much longer. Drew, huffing and puffing and wheezing behind me, must have been regretting his two pack a day habit.

Just then we saw it: providential sanctuary, a blissful, heavenly dark alley on our left. We turned into it and hid behind a dumpster.

"We are so fucked," I said.

"Just relax," said Drew.

I wondered what I would do if a cop came into the alley. Surrender was out of the question; but so was murder. I had no intention of killing anyone. I regretted that I'd had to shoot the hick in the store, but that dumb fuck had really been asking for it. I wondered, *If a cop comes down the alley, will we be able to take him hostage and steal his cop car?* I quickly decided that all the cop cars had GPS transmitters, so stealing one would effectively announce our location to police headquarters.

"Hey," said Drew beside me, "you got a bottle opener?"

We drank some of the stolen beer while we listened to the sirens. From the sound of it, there were two or three squad cars and an ambulance for the guy I shot. If anyone in a passing car had seen us duck into the alley, or if any of the cops had a K-9 unit, then we were likely to be found very soon. A patrol car passed our hiding place, shining a spotlight beam into the alley's shadows. I was grateful that I had worn my black boots; they were clunky to run in, but if I'd worn my lighter weight white tennis shoes, they might have given me away at that moment. As it was, the cop car moved on.

"We gotta get the fuck out of here," I said. Drew nodded his agreement. But where could we go? Breaking into one of the buildings next to the alley would be too noisy; and trying to steal a car while the police searched for us could lead to disaster.

I couldn't think of a better option.

We came out the far end of the alley, and jumped out in front of the first vehicle that came past. The driver slammed on the breaks automatically. I tried to open the driver's door but it was locked.

"Get out of the car before I blow your fucking head off!" I screamed. It was a young woman at the wheel; I even had time to notice that she was kind of cute. She hesitated, clearly wondering if she might still be able to ram Drew, who was standing in front of her car, pointing a gun at her. "Do it! Do it now!" I insisted.

Reluctantly, she put the car in park, unclasped her seat belt, and opened the door. I grabbed her arm and pulled her roughly out.

"Now get the fuck out of here," I told her. She didn't leave though, just stood there looking pissed off.

I climbed behind the wheel and opened the passenger door for Drew. We threw our loot in back and made our escape.

We ditched her car out of town, put our masks in our bags and hid for a couple hours in a darkened park, drinking under some bushes. We found some unknown white powder in the stolen car's glove compartment, which we confiscated on principle, but without knowing what it was, I refused to put it up my nose. Drew had fewer scruples, and was consequently very talkative when he should have been quiet while we were hiding out in the park.

In the morning we rode the city bus back to my apartment.

The whole thing was far too sloppy. Everybody pays with cards these days; we each only got barely a lousy couple hundred bucks from the till at the convenience store.

Most unnervingly, we had very nearly been caught.

Chapter 6

Johnny was a god of vengeance. He had been channeling Mars, the god of war, for so long now that making the transition to Jehovah, the smiting god of destruction, was no great leap for him. He seemed to grow taller and he pronounced his judgment upon us in a booming voice from a wrathful visage twisted by malice that was awful to behold.

"You guys are so fucking stupid!" he raged at Drew and me when he learned of our adventure. "You don't even think about what you're doing. Do you have any idea what the consequences would have been if you had been apprehended?"

"But we weren't caught," objected Drew.

We were all over at Johnny's place, sitting on couches and large armchairs around the low table in the living room, with some of Johnny's whacked-out music playing on the stereo to mask our conversation.

"You got away by a thread," intoned Victor.

"And you would have dragged us down with you," continued Johnny. "Your weapons would have been ID'ed and traced back to the earlier operation. It wouldn't even matter if you talked.

They'd just look at your phone records, conduct a few interviews, watch the surveillance tapes again, and they would figure it all out pretty quickly." He was fighting to keep his voice level, you could tell he really wanted to scream at us. "And then they'd get a couple search warrants, and they would get Victor and me, no doubt about it. Do you understand? If you go down, we go down; and vice versa. We cannot FENCE this shit," he continued in his dangerously quiet voice, "we don't have those kinds of connections, and the cops will have notified the pawn shops to look for us, or for these serial numbers. You get the idea. We can't afford to attract attention."

"If I were a mob boss, I'd totally kill you guys," suggested Victor.

"You really, seriously fucked up," agreed Johnny. "You shot somebody, and all you got out of it was some beer and a couple hundred bucks? That's got to be the stupidest thing I ever heard."

I hung my head in shame. When he put it like that, it really did seem unjustifiably stupid. I couldn't believe that hick had been so bull-headed; and I couldn't believe I had shot him. I had considered this, and told myself that the shooting was justified because if I had not shot him in the leg, then Drew would have shot him in the chest and probably killed him. However, I knew this argument would not earn me any leniency, either from a judge or from Johnny.

"You have to keep in mind the long-term goals of this operation," Johnny was continuing, somewhere outside my head. "If we blow our cover before the engagement, then we'll never get a chance to pull it off. The day of the invasion, well, invading armies typically engage in a certain amount of looting, that's how you pay and feed your army. But before then, seriously, targeted operations only please gentlemen, and even then, only as a group. We are all in this together so the decision to conduct ANY further operations MUST be made unanimously. Are we agreed on this?"

"Agreed," the other three of us said.

"And I just want to say," interjected Victor, "that you guys are a couple of fucking retards."

"Yeah," I mumbled, looking down.

After a pause, Johnny changed the subject. "So it's time to think about the next phase of our operation. What we need is more guns, especially fully automatic rifles, and explosives; maybe a large artillery piece, and if we're lucky, shoulder-fired rockets."

"I didn't see any of those things at the gun shop," I said helpfully.

"And other than some expensive antique automatics, you aren't going to," Johnny affirmed.

"Were you thinking we could find some alternate source, then?" I enquired politely.

"Indeed, it might be possible. There's a gun show coming up," he explained.

"Why would you be able to buy them there, if you can't get them at gun stores?" I asked, perplexed.

"You cruise around, take a spin through the parking lot, you can meet people," explained Victor. "It should be pretty easy."

"But you'd have to have a lot of cash," Johnny finished.

"Okay," I asked, "so where are we going to get that kind of cash?"

"Think classical," said Johnny.

"Like Vivaldi?" I asked.

"Technically, Vivaldi was Baroque," corrected Drew. It was the first thing he'd said in this entire interaction. I looked at him, and he shrugged.

"More like Jesse James," suggested Victor.

Drew got up, and began to light a cigarette next to Johnny's window.

"Hey, I told you, man, you gotta go outside," Johnny yelled.

In the pause, I racked my brain but could only imagine one thing, and it seemed both dangerous and unlikely. Finally I ventured, "You mean, a bank?"

Johnny nodded and said, "A bank."

"There's no other place that keeps the kind of funds we require on the premises," explained Victor.

"But banks are well-guarded," I objected. "I don't think we can just crash a truck through the door in the middle of the night. I mean, none of us know how to crack a vault, right? And as far as I know we don't have explosives to blow the door off."

Johnny shook his head. "They're on our shopping list," he said.

There was only one conclusion. "So, a daytime operation," I said flatly.

The other two nodded. I convulsively drank a few big gulps from my beer.

"We go in with guns drawn," said Victor with relish. Then he said to me, "Not much different from your convenience store."

"We take a teller hostage," said Johnny, "and convince the manager to open the vault. Then we take the money and run."

"And what about their security?" I asked.

"We'll have to screen the location. Not many banks employ on-site armed guards anymore. They all have a button to call the cops. Response times may vary, but you can never count on more than three minutes; in some places, thirty seconds."

"That's not much time," I said doubtfully.

"So we'll need a plan," Johnny answered. "And we have to do it soon. We will need to work under a compressed time scale, now that your little stunt may have potentially blown our cover."

Chapter 7

The next morning, a local contractor was driving to a job site outside town when he saw some masked men pouring gasoline onto a telephone pole. He slowed to look, when suddenly a sedan pulled out onto the road, blocking it. The contractor stopped his truck and shouted through the passenger window, "Hey! What do you think you're doing?"

That's when I jumped out of the sedan, pointed a rifle through the driver's side window of the truck and said, "Put the vehicle in park. Do it slowly. Keep your hands where I can see them. Good. Now slowly unbuckle your seat belt with one hand. Okay. Now, open the door and step out of the vehicle." I backed up so the door would not hit me. The contractor got out of his truck and Victor bound and gagged him with duct tape.

"We gotta get some handcuffs," I said.

Victor made no comment. We put the gagged man in the back seat of the stolen sedan, and rolled it into the ditch. Then Drew flicked his cigarette butt at the telephone pole drenched in gasoline, and walked away as it burst into flames.

Victor got behind the wheel as Johnny, Drew and I climbed into the bed of the truck and lay flat. Victor pulled off his mask for the drive, and instead wore a hooded sweatshirt with a baseball cap and sunglasses, to hide his identity from any pesky surveillance cameras. He obeyed traffic laws, so it took several minutes to drive across the small rural town. We waited in an empty lot down the street from the bank until Victor had seen at least three police cars head towards our distraction at the far end of town. Then he pulled out of the empty lot, down the street, and made a sharp turn that made me roll uncomfortably into the other guys, and finally brought the stolen pickup to a halt right in front of the bank's doors.

The three of us piled out of the bed of the stolen pickup wearing ski masks, each carrying several handguns strapped to our bodies, and big ass guns in our hands. We didn't know if we'd been spotted yet, we didn't even check to see if the bank manager had been able to lock the doors against us by electronic remote control; we just blew away the window glass with a shotgun at close range. A piece of shrapnel or perhaps ricocheting buckshot just missed my ear but I didn't even care.

"Everybody down on the fucking floor!" screamed Drew.

"If nobody does anything stupid, then nobody gets hurt," I called out, as we both waved our weapons. The customers slowly got down on their knees, then stretched face first on the cold tiled floor.

At downtown banks, they keep the tellers behind bulletproof windows. That was why we had selected a nice friendly community bank in a small town some forty minutes away.

Johnny walked straight to the front desk, grabbed one of the frightened tellers and held the muzzle of a handgun to the side of her head.

"Where is the manager?" he shouted.

"I'm the manager," said a man in a suit who was stretched out on the floor.

"Get your ass over here and open the fucking vault," Johnny snapped.

The manager did not argue. I wondered if this had happened to him before. I covered him, Johnny kept his gun on the cashier, and Drew stayed in the lobby for crowd control. The manager led us through a door into the back, then through a very sturdy door locked with a keypad. Inside that room was a monstrous safe. The manager opened the safe with the combination lock and said, "I've complied with your demands. Please don't hurt anyone."

"Shut up and show me where your office is," said Johnny. The manager pointed. Johnny took the manager and the teller to that room, made them empty their pockets and confiscated their cell phones, threw the desk phone into the hallway and stomped on it, then locked them in the office and told them not to waste their lives trying to escape.

Meanwhile I was emptying the contents of the safe into the two duffel bags we had brought along for the purpose. I noticed a flashing red light in one corner of the room and took that to mean the police were already on their way. I worked as fast as I could. Johnny joined me and we wordlessly finished taking everything we could carry. Then we ran back to the lobby, where Drew had moved everyone into a corner on the far side of the room, away from the exit nearest Victor, who was waiting in our getaway car in the parking lot.

But we were too late. A squad car had pulled into the parking lot, blocking our getaway vehicle. Two officers jumped out screaming, "Drop your weapons! Get down on the ground!"

Including Victor there were four of us, well armed, and two of them with semiautomatic pistols and reinforcements presumably around the corner. The three of us exiting the bank quickly spread out and simultaneously fired at the windshield in between the two officers. As it shattered, each of them dropped to the ground behind the open car doors. Then we rushed the police vehicle from both sides, crouching behind parked cars as the officers fired at us.

As I ran through the parking lot, a round caught me full in the chest. It was like getting punched hard, it knocked the wind out of me and I fell down in surprise.

That Kevlar vest was the best thing I ever stole.

In a brief lull Johnny shouted at the police, "We have you surrounded. We don't want to have to hurt you. Drop your weapons."

"We have backup on the way," shouted one of the officers. I could see the other trying to get a clear shot at one of the guys. He didn't know about my vest; he thought I was down, so he wasn't looking at me.

"Well your backup isn't fucking here yet," screamed Johnny, "so if you want to live, drop your fucking weapons right now!"

The cops hesitated, looked at each other. Then out of the corner of my eye I saw Drew approaching the cop car from the rear, partially obscured by a parked pickup truck. The cop closest to me saw this too, and expertly squeezed off five rounds in quick succession, centered on a tight cluster where Drew's head had been only a moment before.

I sprang into a crouch, a handgun in my hand, quickly got to the door and jammed the muzzle against the close-cropped hair on the back of the officer's sweaty head.

"Drop your weapon," I said in a low voice. He hesitated. I heard two of my accomplices rush the cop on the other side of the car, heard his weapon clatter to the ground, heard them locking his hands with his own handcuffs. Still the man at the other end of my gun was holding his own weapon, waiting for me to let down my guard.

"Put it on the ground," I said very slowly, my voice deep and quiet. Reluctantly he complied. I came around to the door, kicked the gun away and said, "Face down on the ground. Now."

All the fight had gone out of him. He was hoping backup would arrive soon. They probably would. It was a miracle they weren't here already. Drew staggered up, looking as shaken and haggard as a masked man ever looked, and helped me cuff the officer. We took his handy accessory belt and his gun and put him in the back seat of the patrol car.

Victor got back behind the wheel of the stolen getaway vehicle. Johnny grabbed the duffel bags full of cash from where I had dropped them when I got shot. The truck was already rolling as we all piled in, and acrid clouds of smoke burned off the tires as Victor peeled out, rammed his way past the cop car, and gunned the truck screaming down the street.

We doubled back to the secluded spot outside town where we had parked our own cars, loaded the money into them, abandoned the stolen car a ways up the road, and we all drove off in different directions.

Chapter 8

After the bank robbery we lay low for a while. I was, if possible, more paranoid than I ever had been before; but in an effort to avoid attracting attention, I finally pulled myself together enough to go out job hunting. I even got an interview at one place, but I was distracted throughout the interview process. I couldn't provide good answers to the stupid questions about the six words my friends would use to describe me, or what my former employers might name as my weaknesses. I kept thinking about how different the interview would be if I were wearing my ski mask and holding a gun. I didn't get the job, which honestly surprised me because I thought I was more than qualified for the position: so I took out a cash advance on my credit card so I could pay the rent without using stolen money. In a sense, this seemed counterintuitive; but I never intended to pay off my credit card, at this point; and I figured this would confuse anyone who might be watching my financial activity, and perhaps convince them that I was not involved in the bank robbery. Through my veil of paranoia I was hopeful, and this enabled me to get up in the morning.

We had agreed beforehand that we would use our haul from the robbery to fund the growth of our army. All of the brand new bills went to the growth fund: we knew that the serial numbers would be traceable, so they would best be spent on the black market as soon as possible. All the assorted other bills that had already been used could be spent on anything at all.

"How much did we get?" I asked.

"A lot," said Victor, counting bills with Johnny.

"How much do we need?" I pressed.

"At least twice as much."

Still, it was enough to get started; so, flush with stolen cash, Victor and Johnny went to a gun show in search of weapons.

At the legitimate booths they bought sundries including high-powered scopes, night vision goggles, knives, mace, handcuffs, tear gas canisters, long-range walkie-talkies, a police band scanner, radar detectors, and some really awful chili.

More importantly, Johnny and Victor met Ramon in the parking lot outside the gun show. Ramon was half black, half Mexican, and he claimed to know everyone and to have access to anything.

Victor later related the encounter to Drew and me, as we passed around the bong back in Johnny's living room.

"So we're walking through the parking lot, sort of cruising around, and this guy who we'd seen inside the show was sort of hanging around next to a pickup truck, and he's all, 'hey what up,' and we're like, 'yo,' so he goes, 'what you fellas up to?' And we're just like, 'cruisin' around,' you know, playin' it cool, and so he goes, 'are you gentlemen interested in making a purchase?' And Johnny's just like, 'Possibly, it depends on what you have in stock.' And this guy just goes, 'whatever you need,' and Johnny's like, 'you have it with you?' and this guy points inside the canopy of his truck and there are all these crates, and he's like, 'fully automatics, ammo, explosives,' and I'm thinking like, jackpot, right, but Johnny's just like, 'we might be interested in inspecting the merchandise, but perhaps we should continue this conversation in a more discreet location?' So we get in our cars and we follow this guy through the industrial district and park in front of some abandoned shed and this guy Ramon opens a crate for us and sure enough, bam, M-16's, lots of them; and not rusty mismatched antiques either, we're talking brand-new military-grade equipment here. So Johnny just calmly makes a cash offer, and before I know it the whole deal is done, we move the crates, the cash changes hands, and then the guy's like, 'it's a pleasure doing business with you, and here's my card if you want anything else.'

The card was handwritten, with just a first name and a cell phone number. It wasn't long before Johnny called the number and set up a meeting to discuss the possibility of future business arrangements. We were all in the room watching when he made the call. The line seemed to have been ringing for a long time; Johnny was just about to make a comment and hang up, when a look of surprise crossed his face and he said, "Yeah, uh, hello! My name's Johnny, is this Ramon? Yeah, I met you at the gun show, and I was wondering if we could discuss, uh, some things. What? Oh, no, no problems at all. We're very happy. Sure, tomorrow is fine. Uh, we usually get together at the shitty dirty tavern down the street. Piss Beer, you know the one?" He told him the address. "What time works for you? All right, see you then."

He hung up the phone and looked at us. "Tomorrow afternoon at the bar."

Ramon, when he got there, appeared very relaxed. He introduced his companion as Lamont, and we introduced ourselves and everybody shook hands all the way around. To put us at ease, Ramon then chatted gregariously for a few minutes about sports and women before turning the subject to the business matter at hand.

"So, what exactly are you fellows looking for?" he asked casually. His companion leaned forward keenly. My pulse quickened, and I felt my face begin to flush.

"More of the same," answered Johnny in a low voice that I could barely make out over the background noise, "and some other stuff too."

Ramon leaned closer to Johnny and said in an equally low voice, "Like what?"

Johnny pitched his voice so quiet that only Ramon could hear him, but I could see him ticking off items on his fingers, as though there were a fairly extensive list.

Ramon nodded wordlessly as Johnny made this recital, and the expression on his face appeared for all the world like the highly skilled maitre d' at an upscale restaurant who never writes down orders but remembers them all perfectly.

There was a pause, and then I heard Johnny ask quietly, "So, how much are we looking at, for all that?"

"A lot," said Ramon.

Johnny raised his eyebrows expectantly.

Ramon leaned in and said something quietly that made Johnny's brows furrow. At length Johnny said, "You might have to give us a few weeks to come up with it."

Ramon's face broke into a huge grin. "No problem. I like doing business with you guys. There's no bullshit." He appeared to think for a moment, and then nonchalantly dropped a bomb. "By the way," said he, "you guys must be hunting some big game."

We had not tried to offer any explanation as to why we wanted all these weapons. This notion that we might be hunters was clearly a ruse which he would know that we would see through. *How far can we trust this guy?* I wondered. The others must have been thinking the same thing because there was an uncomfortable silence where nobody said anything for a very long second.

Then Johnny said, "Pretty big."

I took a big gulp of my beer.

"Well," said Ramon, "maybe you should come back to my place and we can talk more about it."

None of us said anything.

"Come on guys," said Ramon in a low voice. Everybody leaned their heads in towards the center of the table to hear. "I'm not going to rat you out. If I wanted to do that, I could do it already. It's more likely that you guys would rat me out, but I did a little background check on these two," he indicated Victor and Johnny, who both looked a bit surprised, "and you are both in the clear with no known police involvement, so I'm willing to talk things over, although maybe we should go someplace where we won't have to talk so quietly. Now look," he continued before anyone could interrupt, "you wouldn't need this much gear unless you were outfitting a lot of guys. It stands to reason you're planning a pretty big hunting party. Now, I don't know you dudes too well, but I'd be willing to bet money that you haven't yet filled all the positions for your little excursion; and that being the case, I might be able to help you out." He paused for emphasis. We were all ears. "I know a lot of people," he continued. "It's just possible I might know some hunters who would be interested in going on an expedition." He paused again, turned to Johnny and said just barely loud enough that we could all hear, "And if you cut me in on the stake, I might be able to cut you a deal on your supplies."

Johnny nodded slowly and said, "You're right. Maybe we should continue this conversation someplace more private."

Ramon and his "hunters" did not fuck around. They understood our project very well from the beginning and although it may have originally been our idea, I don't think we could have even attempted to carry it off without them.

Our haul from the first bank robbery was barely enough to pay for a couple crates of guns and ammunition. Our end goal would require more weapons, more ammo, and a lot more guys. We needed time to recruit new members. We needed money to afford to bide our time, and we needed money to buy more weapons.

So we pulled another heist.

We all rode in the back of a generic white utility van; a stolen vehicle, of course. Victor pulled right up to the front door of the bank and the forward team jumped out with our masks on, dressed in black, wearing black ski masks and latex gloves, carrying automatic rifles. Lamont stationed guards at all the entrances and exits to the property, in case the police again arrived before the holdup was concluded. Meanwhile five of us burst through the doors of the bank and immediately threw several flash grenades that Lamont had concocted from old fireworks. They were remarkably effective, so dazzling that they blinded even those of us who knew what was going on.

The people in the bank lobby were completely stunned. One moment they were standing there, going about their business; the next moment there was a blinding flash of light, and the bank lobby filled with smoke, and the terrifying sound of gunshots at close proximity (I fired a few rounds at the ceiling to get everyone's attention – it was incredibly loud in the enclosed space) and next thing they knew they were surrounded by masked, sort of Special Ops looking paramilitary men pointing guns at their heads and screaming "Get the fuck down on the floor! Do it now, before I blow your fucking head off!"

I was on crowd control with Drew and another of Ramon's guys. We were in charge of doing the shouting. Ramon and Johnny were the ones who took the teller and the manager hostage and went back to the vault with them and returned with duffel bags full of cash. It all went very quickly, and after the first few seconds I hardly had to do anything. I just watched people lying on the floor and occasionally kicked them to encourage them not to move.

The difference from the first bank robbery was that this bank was in the middle of a major metropolitan area. Four police cars arrived right away. Those tellers are quick with that button, I swear. Maybe one of them pressed it with her knee.

As soon as those four cop cars came into view, Lamont and his guard team began shooting at them. They kept an almost continuous stream of rifle fire aimed at each squad car, which made it difficult for the police to come to a stop near the bank. Instead they used their vehicles to blockade the street at either end of the block, cutting off our escape. The cops got out of their vehicles, crouched behind them, and returned fire towards Lamont and his team.

That was when Drew grabbed some random woman by her shirt collar and physically hauled her off the bank lobby floor. She struggled at first, so he whacked her on the head with the butt of his pistol; she settled down a bit after that. With one arm around her neck practically choking her, he put the gun to the side of her head and, holding her in front of him, stepped out the door of the bank. The firefight between Lamont's team and the police continued for a few more heart-pounding moments before they comprehended the hostage situation and one of the officers shouted, "Hold your fire!"

The impasse continued for far too long, Drew with his hostage, the police with their guns, as we waited for Johnny and Ramon to get done with the vault. After what seemed like weeks, the two of them finally emerged with their duffel bags. I resisted the urge to ask them if they had been off on honeymoon. Instead I imitated Drew by grabbing a hostage, a skinny old Chinese man, and holding a gun at his temple. "Move and you die," I told him, "do you understand?" He nodded mutely. I held him in front of me and walked out the door with the rest behind me.

"Release the hostages," shouted one of the police officers. "We cannot let you take them with you."

"Shut up or we kill them," shouted Ramon. Holding a hostage between ourselves and the police on either side of our group, we piled into the waiting van. Victor looked grim as he put it into gear and began rolling before we were all inside. I was the last one. I refused to be left behind. I gave the old man a hard shove with my foot and sent him sprawling as I dove into the van. Someone slammed the rolling door shut behind me and the van lurched into gear.

Victor was driving straight towards the police cars that were blocking the street. As we approached, Lamont pulled the pin out of a military issue grenade and tossed it under one of the cop cars; then pulled the pin out of another grenade and tossed it under the other cop car. The officers ran for cover. The explosion was impressive, but hardly sufficient to demolish the police cars. Instead Victor stepped on the gas and rammed them; but those squad cars are heavy, and the van was surprisingly pathetic. We didn't quite break through the first time, and he had to put the van in reverse and ram them again; but then miraculously, with a great grinding of metal, we were past the roadblock and driving on.

It didn't take more than a few seconds before the other two police cars were right behind us, sirens wailing. We waited until an appropriate moment, then opened up the back doors of the van and showed our hostage to the lead vehicle. The squad car's driver slowed, momentarily, and we took that moment to throw our screaming hostage out the back door of the speeding van. The police cars had to slam on their brakes to avoid running her over. Victor sped up, turned a corner, ran a red light, smashed into a little Toyota at full speed and sent it spinning across the intersection.

The utility van was still functional, so he floored the gas and drove back to the place where we had stowed our own vehicles.

As we came to a stop we checked to make sure the coast was clear, and then emerged from the van without our ski masks, loaded the loot into our waiting cars, and sped off into the sunset.

Chapter 9

After the second bank robbery, Victor and Johnny moved into a farmhouse outside town. Of course, Drew and I were there all the time, and often Ramon and Lamont and their friends would show up with their girls and lots of drugs and beer.

Ramon was an essential contact. Not only was he able to supply our nascent militia with its requisite armaments, but the dude really did know everybody and have access to everything. Through him we were able to gain the one thing we needed more than anything else: new recruits.

Recruiting had been the subject of much discussion and controversy. We required a large fighting force to accomplish our objective, but how could we recruit members without exposing ourselves? Our very lives depended upon the secrecy of our plan. The recruits could not be told the final objective until they had passed some kind of initiation, nor could anyone be informed of any concrete plan until the group was en route to carrying it out.

We tried to work up a psychological profile of our most promising prospects for recruitment, and discussed recruitment strategies and techniques.

We considered all the possibilities and discussed them ad nauseam. The back-and-forth went on for weeks, and more than once grew quite heated.

In particular, we initially disagreed about the hot-button topic of whether or not we should recruit women. After all, Chuck Palahniuk made *Fight Club* an all-male organization. The question created some tension within our group.

"You see," Johnny tried to explain his logic to us when we were out at the bar one night, "I tend to think of women as being more, I don't know, let's say *idealistic*, for lack of a better word. It's my impression that women tend to be more idealistic than men; which is why my initial thought was that we should avoid recruiting women into the Hillsboro Militia project: because if they're idealists, then they would be much *less* likely to agree to participate in such a fundamentally nihilistic and violent association; and therefore they would be far *more* likely to rat us out to the authorities. Or if they did join, they would want to turn this whole operation into some kind of neo-Marxist postmodernist crusade against reality: and I think I would rather get ratted out to the police than have to pretend to endorse that kind of bullshit. That's why, in general, I see women as much riskier potential recruits. But on the other hand, women have proven themselves on the battlefield in modern times, again and again, from Iraq to Ukraine and beyond. So maybe we just need to figure out how to screen them properly, to keep the nuts out. I don't know. I'm trying to figure this one out. We're all equal, but we're not all the same. Discuss."

"Women don't approve of violence," Victor claimed immediately.

"Except when they do," Drew interjected.

"Women are gentle, kind, compassionate, caring, and loving," Victor continued, perpetuating a popular stereotype.

"Except when they're not," Drew reminded us.

"We can't ask women to go out and shoot random strangers in the name of our pointless power play," Victor insisted. "It would be morally wrong."

Well, everything about our entire plan was morally wrong, really; but I thought I might be able to offer a more nuanced perspective on this point. "Women are human beings," I began. "Some are angels, and some are assholes, but most are just..." I shrugged. "People," I concluded. Then I lowered my voice because I didn't want to include total strangers in this discussion. "However, our combat training exercises might get pretty rough," I said, considering how all this might play out. "That could get really awkward for our trainees, when it's time to learn how to fight: because it's shameful to hurt women. Nobody will want to fight them, unless we split the classes, or–"

"Y'all do what you want," opined Ramon, "but life without the ladies is too fuckin' gay for me. I mean, it's fine with me if you prefer dick, that don't bother me none; but personally, I like the pussy. And as for training? I'd much rather grapple with a girl, naamsayin?"

"White women fetishize Black men," Lamont stated bluntly. "That works out pretty well for me, so I think we should include them."

"You guys are only thinking about sex," corrected Johnny. "That's not the point here. Obviously we're going to have women over at the house, are you kidding? Have you even been there? No, the question is whether we should recruit them into an insurrectionist militia, hand them guns, and involve them in our decision-making process."

"The Battle of Hillsboro represents a quest for ultimate freedom," Drew dissented, "but there's no real freedom if we get women involved: because women never get tired of telling you what to do."

There was a shocked silence for a moment. A woman at the next table glared deadly daggers at Drew, she must have overheard him.

"Not all women!" said Victor, perhaps hoping to mollify the woman at the neighboring table.

"They never fuckin' stop telling you what you're allowed to say," Drew continued even more loudly, apparently hoping to cause offense.

"Not all women!" Victor repeated, looking embarrassed to be seen in the company of such a misogynist male chauvinist pig.

"And they never, ever stop telling you that you have it so much better than them," Drew concluded, ignoring Victor. "Bitch, you ain't lived my life, you don't know shit about me, stop telling me what I've lived through. Fuckin' spoiled princess with a fluffy pillow and a stuffed unicorn griping at me about how 'oppressed' she is while I work for minimum wage doing dirty, sweaty manual labor."

"Not all –" Victor began.

"Shut the fuck up with your 'not all women,'" Drew snapped. "This ain't social media."

"Be that as it may," Johnny reminded us, "we need as many recruits as we can get. The more I think about this, the more obvious the conclusion seems. It doesn't matter what our potential recruits look like, so long as they share our primary objective."

"And a woman can fire a rifle just as well as a man," I reminded my companions, in an apparent reversal of my earlier position. "I grew up out in the country, I've seen women shoot – "

"Fine," grumbled Drew, interrupting me. "But if I hear anyone utter the word 'patriarchy,' I swear I'll..." Drew's empty threat was drowned out by a new hit song blaring from the juke box, a song in which a woman who presented herself as a gentle, kind, and caring victim sang sweetly about how all men are manipulative jerks and worthless liars who deserve to get viciously stomped.

Thus we finally agreed to accept recruits without consideration of gender. Even so, generally speaking we were most actively looking for males between 17 and maybe 34 years old. We agreed that certain criminal backgrounds were acceptable or even desirable; while others were contrary to our target profile. Our ideal prospect would have a minimum of education, no accumulated wealth, little or no present employment, and few close personal connections. In other words, we were looking for people who were hopeless and resentful, so we could exploit their psychology of victimhood by offering their lives meaning and purpose through pointless violence. However, we ourselves did not entirely fit this profile: since we were all college educated, and at the outset of these escapades we were all more or less employed. The discrepancy gave rise to the obvious objection: if we ourselves don't fit the profile, what good is the profile, and what's a better one? But we couldn't come up with a better one, so we used it as a general rule of thumb and made frequent exceptions. For example, we permitted some recruits who possessed personal wealth in the form of expensive cars; and there were a few who we let in against our better judgment even though they had kids; and we were surprised at how frequently we made our most common exception, which was for education.

A better educated gang of thugs has never been assembled on this earth.

We very systematically set about recruiting members. We would usually meet one person through another acquaintance, and then we kept track of them carefully. We employed CRM business software designed for salespeople. We set up a database of contacts and leads, and stored as much information as we could obtain about each individual: their name, age, race, gender, sexual preference, relationship status, employment status, housing status, financial status, criminal history, present criminal involvement, known associates. You could click on the known associates to view their profiles. The software featured an integrated calendar. We could keep track of how recently each person had been contacted and implement an auto notification system to remind us to attempt to contact tagged persons of interest for follow-up. After a first visit, call them back a few days later. Follow up a week after that and then three weeks after that.

In the process, the hangout pad became party central.

We didn't want to get too deeply involved with anyone until we had met them in person; but getting the prospective recruits to come over to our house was not a problem.

We always had a party going on. There were women, there was booze, and there were fantastic drugs being passed around more or less constantly. People are naturally attracted to a permanent party. You get cycles where a certain small number of individuals form a semi-permanent fixture; then those people rotate out and some different people come over all the time. Throughout, there is a constant stream of random stragglers: the disconnected wanderers, the antisocials, or conversely, the swinging socialites and busy urbanites who pass through briefly, always on their way somewhere else.

The frequent attendees fell into two categories. Some were trusted lieutenants who had undergone initiation rites and who, over a period of time, were assigned regular roles and responsibilities within our organization, such as finding more recruits. The rest were completely excluded from the inner workings of our group; they were the hangers-on who legitimized our scene, because they really knew nothing, so if they had been interrogated they could not link us to any criminal activity.

It was this fringe group of disconnected infrequent attendees that proved the best resource for new recruits. When a new person who we didn't know showed up at a party, we made them feel welcome, plied them with drinks, kept them involved in conversation until they looked tipsy, then we gradually, tactfully elicited a host of detailed personal information. By the end of the evening many of these new arrivals felt that whichever of us had been assigned to their interrogation was their new best friend, and they gladly provided detailed and accurate contact information and personal histories.

Having boiled down the essence of what we knew about a person, we thoroughly vetted them on the Internet. It's amazing what you can find out about a person if you know a couple of basic details about them. It's complicated, though, because the kinds of people we were researching were often already accustomed to covering their tracks online, using VPNs and sock puppet accounts and whatnot so their bad behavior couldn't easily be traced back to them. And it's even more complicated when you're trying to look up someone with a common name like Jones, because it turns out there are countless other people with exactly the same name, and it's easy to jump to false conclusions.

Assuming the prospect met our basic criteria, a few days or a week later we would call the person and invite them to another event, where there were always a lot of hot chicks. And remember: women like going to parties where there are other women. There's a multiplier effect. A few well-placed invitations early on paid off unbelievably over time.

After that, if our prospect didn't become regulars at our party house right away, we would contact them once every couple weeks, and they showed up every time. We would continue to contact them until either they asked us about the initiation, or they ceased to fit our target profile. Most of them soon asked about initiation.

Ramon's gang was not required to go through initiation, but all other new recruits had to do something of a criminal and financially rewarding nature, to prove their devotion to our nihilist philosophy. Initiates who passed this test were asked if they wanted to help start a war. They all said yes without asking for any explanation; for after all, who cares *why* we were starting a war? "Why" is such a tedious detail. Wars are for starting! That was enough. The recruits agreed, without exception; which was good, because if any had refused, we would have had to make some difficult choices. We told the recruits to remain on standby and that they could be called up at any time. We told them to procure a ski mask or a hockey mask or at least a bandanna, and some black clothes with no identifying markings.

We did not have access to a firing range or appropriate training grounds. The farmhouse where we partied was not nearly remote enough for automatic weapons fire. We were rightly concerned that, if we all met up at some remote location to test fire our automatic rifles, we would be certain to draw the attention of Homeland Security or some anti-terrorism task force.

Instead, our weapons training was conducted quietly, in small groups, without actually discharging our weapons. We learned and then showed others how to take apart and clean our automatic rifles, how to reload them, and how to aim.

On this last point I interrupted the proceedings and stood up to make an announcement. "You don't shoot from the hip like they do in the movies," I said. "A wild spray of bullets does not increase your chances of hitting your target. Take careful aim before you pull the trigger. Fire short bursts, then stop, reassess the situation, and aim again before you continue firing. Otherwise, you waste bullets, you give away your position, and you wind up dead. So remember, three to five round bursts, unless you're in a really heavy firefight."

I know that people hearing my story will say, "Oh, it was the drugs," as though that explained everything: it must have been the drugs that made us go crazy and decide to do all this fucked up shit. But the drugs were really just something to do while we waited. We couldn't have training camps because they would be noticed, so we just had a party. The drugs helped to pass the time while we procured our figurative chess pieces and moved them into position. We had to develop an intricate structure of networked support, with groups of pawns backing each other up and providing general stability for our central plan.

All this took a lot of time, as it turned out; and in the meanwhile the availability of drugs at our parties helped to recruit certain types of people who were into that sort of thing. Sometimes being able to cackle hysterically at the way someone else's laugh sounds can really help to pass the time. Fortunately the parties were good enough that the drugs did not completely repel people who weren't into them: the rockabilly greasers and some of the straight-edge tattoos-n-piercings crowd found enough of each other at our gatherings that we were able to keep them coming back despite their disinterest in some of our primary proclivities at that time.

And the drugs didn't make us much money, either. We only sold to a small group of close friends, and the money didn't even cover the cost of all the shit we simply gave away for free at our parties. But this generosity won us many new friends.

We weren't interested in selling drugs as a business activity. We did not want to get drawn into the paltry economics of petty drug dealing and turf wars with rival gangs. We were playing for bigger stakes.

I don't even credit the drugs with preventing us from thinking about what we were doing and its implications for our own future. We were planning the whole thing very carefully for a single purpose; and after that, hey, we would see what happened. We were like a child who builds an elaborate, time-consuming and well-thought-out contraption to stand on, just so he can poke his finger into a wasp's nest. The purpose of our labors was to attempt some insane stunt; and this gave our lives meaning. It was like being evil Clark Kent going to work every day but knowing that underneath it all you're secretly evil Superman. We were more than just the mild-mannered couple of guys we appeared to be. Secretly, we were plotting to take over for real.

It was screamin' scary fun to be the bad guy. It was so scary that we tried not to think about the scary part. We did what we could to keep our operations on the down-low, and then just focused on the day to day protocols and procedures which had to be undertaken conducted and maintained in order for us to accomplish our primary overarching objectives.

If some hypothetical criminologist or psychological profiler or whatever were to assign a motive to my actions, they might speculate that perhaps I turned to violence because, although I thirsted for power, I had not the skills to become a politician.

It is true that a good politician should be able to quickly remember the names of a large number of people, because this tricks people into thinking that the politician truly, deeply cares about them as an individual; whereas I could never remember anyone's name, and just smiled and addressed them as "you" or "dude" even when they pointedly addressed me by my own name, which was awkward, but what do I look like, a fucking encyclopedia of who's who in Loserville?

Furthermore, it is true that a good politician should be a skilled rhetorician, able to either forcefully state a position or just as forcefully dodge a question and to be able to expound upon that dodge at length, loudly and voluminously, on and on until you have no idea what the fuck they're going on about; whereas I, on the other hand, rather tended to mumble, and to stumble over my words, and to speak so slowly that other people would often butt in and talk over me. Depending on your perspective, you might say that my motivation was somewhat different from that of a politician.

Like any political figure throughout history, since times so ancient and lost in the forgotten mist of history that the very existence of their cities and their tyrants can now only be deduced from translated inscriptions on scraps of crumbling masonry, or from a passing reference in the oral history of a neighboring civilization; since before even these ancient kings, throughout the history of humanity, all the way up to the modern era with our so-called democratic ideals and – oh my god don't get me started about all that shit – like any of these figures throughout the history of humanity, my friends and I desired power. It was that simple. Like any political figure through history, we wanted to rule and control.

But make no mistake, there were tremendous differences in our approach. Unlike modern politicians, we had decided to obtain power without mucking about with negative advertising and industry lobbyists and all the daily polls of certain target demographics. Unlike most modern politicians, we never pretended either to ourselves or to our key constituents that we had any intention of making the world a better place for anyone.

Nothing could have been farther from our minds. We wanted to enrich ourselves at the expense of others; just like pirates, or banks. We did not have any pretensions of making anything better for anyone else. On top of that, we wanted to take over a real city, just like our video game characters would go take over a city in the latest generation high resolution interactive character and first person shooter video games.

We thought it would be fun.

But of course, it wasn't all about fun, was it. No, it was about anger, too. As I looked at my life in those days after we first hatched our little scheme, I saw that I was directionless, hopeless, useless, and completely dissatisfied with everything I had fucked up in my pointless life.

Things hadn't worked out the way I always thought they were supposed to. What the fuck was up with that? I always thought my life would turn out like a Hollywood movie with a happy ending. I always thought I'd get out of high school and I would turn out to be better and smarter than everyone else, and that would make me rich and famous by the time I was in my mid-twenties, like Bill Gates. That was my plan. I didn't even really want to be famous, but I saw it as a necessary evil counterpart to wealth, and I was willing to put up with the fame, more or less, so long as I could be really and truly stinking rich.

But fame didn't turn out to be my necessary evil. Instead I got stuck with roommates. Roommates were the necessary evil I had to put up with, in my mid-twenties, until I finally decided that I hated roommates more than I hated anything, even more than I hated the rapper Eminem, or the state of Texas, or my psychotic ex-girlfriend: put the three together, and roommates are worse; and so I lied about my income on the rental application for an apartment, just so I could get away from those assholes. One might posit that the financial hardship I endured on account of the disproportionate percentage of my income I was thereafter compelled to pay in rent might have been one of the factors which eventually drove me to my life of crime; yet I suspect that even if I had still been living with roommates on that night when my friends and I had that first conversation at the bar and dreamed up our whole scheme, events still would have played out along similar lines.

Because the fact is that I was angry. I had been told that this was the land of opportunity, but all the opportunities seemed to have passed me by, and I thought maybe it was time I should finally take matters into my own hands.

See, I was the kid in high school who would steel up the nerve to ask a girl to "go out with me," only to be told, "You're nice, but…" Then when I got a little older, the girls used to dump me saying, "You're a real nice guy, but…" One of them even told me bluntly, "You're too nice." She actually seemed kind of mad about it. I couldn't understand. I just knew that I'd had enough.

I was sick of being nice. I was sick of having a job where I had to be nice to people instead of punching them in the face. More than anything else, I was sick of people. I was sick of people who interrupt you and talk over you and disrespect you and talk shit about you behind your back or even straight to your face for no reason. I was sick of people who drive behind you with their high beams on, sick of people who cut you off with their shopping cart in the supermarket, sick of people who talk too loud in small restaurants, sick of yuppies, sick of rednecks, sick of the news, sick of advertisements, fucking sick of fucking everyone and all their fucking bullshit.

Fuck them.

They made me want to shoot people.

Thus it was, in my mind, because of "people" that, in the end, I felt totally comfortable with my role in the events outlined here.

It didn't really matter who the actual people were, or what might happen to them once we invaded their town. On some level, I figured, whatever happened, it served them right.

Well, actually I did have a pang of guilt, and voiced my concerns (that we should avoid civilian casualties, and that we must not molest any women) to my companions repeatedly, in hopes that by raising these concerns I would somehow expiate my latent guilt; until finally Victor was like, "All right, we fucking get it dude, we will only rape the willing and the dead," a comment so tasteless that it made everyone laugh, and made clear to me that I had over-pressed my point.

That was about the extent of my efforts to mitigate my actions. I did not, for example, renounce the conspiracy, or attempt to dissuade my companions, or turn myself in to the police, or just sort of drift away disinterestedly like I had done with everything else in my life. Any of these actions might have more or less exonerated me and could almost certainly have prevented many terrible things from happening; but that's not what I did, because that's not who I was.

Instead, I actively participated in the planning and execution of I don't know how many felonies, not the least of which might have been something along the lines of "Recruiting members into a domestic terrorist organization," if I had ever gone to court.

I'm glad I never had to go to court.

It would have been boring.

Chapter 10

One night when we were tripping our faces off in the living room at the farmhouse, we started reading to each other out of the classics. We had not intended to have a literary reading, it was just another bizarre adventure we had during the course of an evening. There was a pile of books on the coffee table in the middle of the room; Johnny had filled them with sticky-note place markers, and had highlighted underlined or outlined certain passages as well.

I don't recall what began the conversation, but somehow I found myself explaining why I thought we would be able to accomplish our invasion of a small town without firing a single shot. "You just show up with massive force," I proposed, "you overwhelm them completely so that they give up rather than try to attempt the futility of fighting back. They just see there are too many of us and we are too well-armed and they will just go limp and placid."

Nobody said anything for a few moments, and then my friends all took turns telling me that I was nuts.

"You think they will just go limp, huh?" asked Victor.

"Well, yeah, sure, if we show up with enough manpower."

"How much manpower would that be?" asked Drew.

"I don't know. A lot."

"And you think if we had enough guys that we could just march in there and take over and we wouldn't have to kill anybody," Victor reiterated.

"Well, yeah," I said defensively.

"Dude," Johnny told me patronizingly, "I'm sorry but that's just not how it's done."

"Let's see," said Drew, and picked up a large book from the bottom of the pile, scattering the other books all over the floor, to cries of protest from Johnny, which Drew appeared not to notice.

The book he had retrieved turned out to be *The Iliad* of Homer, that great and ancient work of Western Literature: a work that is, above all else, a tale of war. Drew opened it to one of the bookmarks at random, scanned the page and began reading: "Nestor in a great voice cried out to the men of Argos: 'O beloved Danaan fighters, henchmen of Ares, let no man any more hang back with his eye on the plunder designing to take all the spoil he can gather back to the vessels; let us kill the men now, and afterwards at your leisure all along the plain you can plunder the corpses.'" He paused for effect and snapped the book shut. "I think that's pretty clear," he opined. "That's how it's done."

I was not prepared to kill a person. In retrospect this sounds illogical: our stated premise had always been military invasion and control, and no military invasion in history has ever been accomplished without loss of life. You don't become a Julius Caesar, a Genghis Khan, or an Alexander the Great without resorting to a certain degree of ruthlessness. My hope that we could pull off our operation without bloodshed may seem irrational; perhaps just as insane as the very idea of invading a nearby town. Certainly none of my companions had encouraged me to think we could accomplish this peacefully. We had simply never discussed it specifically, the loss of life; and in this way, I had allowed myself to persist in the logical fallacy that all our guns were just for show.

I grabbed for another book, *The Art of War* by Sun Tzu. Initially I had trouble focusing my eyes, but I soon flipped to a certain passage, and read out in my own defense, "Sun Tzu said: Generally in war the best policy is to take a state intact; to ruin it is inferior to this. To win one hundred victories in one hundred battles is not the acme of skill. To subdue the enemy without fighting is the acme of skill."

"Yes, but how do you propose to take the town without fighting?" pressed Johnny.

"With a bunch of guys, like I said," I answered, feeling I had already won this argument and my friends were just too dense to see it.

"How many guys does Sun Tzu say you will need?"

I flipped to the relevant page and read, "A thousand attack chariots, a thousand armored wagons, and one hundred thousand mailed troops." I skipped down a bit. "The cost will amount to one thousand pieces of gold a day. After this money is in hand, one hundred thousand troops may be raised."

"You see there our dilemma," Drew observed.

"There's no way we can possibly get together that many guys," said Victor.

"And that's mostly because we don't have nearly that amount of money," concluded Johnny.

I had thought we'd be able to get together that many guys. Okay, I hadn't thought about it at all. I had made whatever assumptions were required to tell myself that the plans we were making weren't really that bad.

"How much does a piece of gold weigh?" I asked brightly.

"Why?" asked Victor.

"Well, we could figure out the value based on the current price of gold per ounce, and then we would know how much money we need." Looking around I sensed belatedly that something was amiss with my comment.

"That's not the point," explained Johnny impatiently. "The point is that it's more money than we are going to get by robbing a couple of banks. It's the kind of money that only governments and multinational corporations have access to. The overwhelming force, 'Shock and Awe' strategy is simply not going to work for adventurers in our situation.

"Instead, we are going to utilize the urban warfare tactics employed so successfully by Hamas when they took over the Gaza Strip from Fatah a few years back, do you remember that?"

"Yeah," I said, "and more recently there were those Pakistani Special Forces guys who killed all those people in Mumbai."

"That was just stupid," remarked Drew.

"They didn't even get any money, and they all died," said Victor in agreement. He and Drew drunkenly clinked glasses. I was glad to see them getting along.

"Some of their tactics were sound, though," mused Johnny. "For example, they brought along bags of almonds for energy, as well as GPS units and detailed maps to find their way around."

"They were in communication by cell phone with a controller at a remote location who had computer access," I remembered.

"Well, we're not going to follow their strategy that closely," said Johnny.

"Where we're going, we probably won't get very good cell phone service," said Victor.

"Anyway," said Drew, "are you going to give up on your hippie pacifism, or do we have to lock you in the broom closet?"

"Ha ha," I said, wondering if they really would. They might try. *Fuck them*, I thought, my hand creeping towards the gun in my pocket.

I had no illusions that I was a "good person," before all this began. Certainly I would not have described myself as entirely a "bad person" or "evil," either; but I was no angel. Nobody is perfect. I told lies sometimes; I drove recklessly sometimes; and I occasionally purloined the odd unwatched knick-knack or thingamajig. I am not so different from everyone else.

Giving myself over to the insane idea of mounting a military invasion against a nearby small town had been completely liberating. The very concept was so utterly ridiculous that I could feel legitimately that I had severed my last remaining ties to the commonly understood condition of reality. Some might say I had disconnected from my sanity, but I felt no less lucid or rational than before. And the reason I felt so free, having severed these ties, was that through the act of severing my ties to the common perception of reality, I had finally succeeded in cutting away my guilt.

I didn't feel at all bad about what we were doing. Once you have declared yourself a military invader, the normal rules of morality no longer apply. Dostoevsky wrote, "Whoever is strong in mind and spirit will have power over men. Anyone who is greatly daring is right in their eyes. He who despises most things will be a law-giver among them and he who dares most of all will be most in the right! So it has been till now and so it will always be." This is why insurgencies are so difficult to quell. This was going to be how our little group would attract a following and grow to be a large army. All we had to do was look mean, and our minions would come running. Once we killed a bunch of people, our popularity would snowball.

Yet despite all this, I remained committed, deep in some schizophrenic part of my inner core, to the idea of mounting a bloodless coup. For some reason, I really thought we would be able to pull this off. My hope was that if we were able to raise a sufficient size force, armed with sufficient munitions, we could march into a small town and occupy it indefinitely without having to fire a shot, or at least not until the first SWAT team arrived.

I didn't think much beyond the first SWAT team. I suppose I thought that we would be able to take so many hostages that the authorities would not dare cross our barricades. Our tactics until now had essentially relied upon similar threats which were not carried out. We had robbed two banks, a convenience store and a gun store, and stolen at least half a dozen cars, several from their owners at gunpoint, all with only one injured and nobody killed. I felt supremely confident that we could maintain this track record even as our operation escalated in scope. It was all a question of tactics and preparation, I told myself.

"Well, let's see what Sun Tzu says about commanding a smaller force," I said. I found a passage and read aloud, "Uh... be capable of eluding the enemy, for a small force is but booty for one more powerful." I looked up and summarized, "Shit."

"Basically," Johnny extrapolated, "in this passage, Sun Tzu is describing the tactics which militias employ in Iraq and Afghanistan. Those are the kinds of tactics that we shall adopt: the time-honored tactic of guerilla warfare, taking our lessons from the strategies we see in the daily news used by militant groups like the Taliban, Hamas, and Hezbollah."

I thought about this for a moment. "Dude," I said, "I'm not into suicide bombing. You want to blow yourself up, whatever, but…"

"At least we will be taking out strictly legitimate targets," said Victor.

"Not ordinary civilians," explained Johnny.

I had the feeling I was missing something. "Are we really going to set off a bomb?" I asked.

"Where have you been dude?" asked Victor.

"We were just talking about that!" laughed Drew.

Now I remembered: that was how this conversation had started. I was so deeply in denial that I had completely blocked it from my mind.

"Listen," said Johnny. "This is Machiavelli." And he read, "The Romans were compelled to lay waste many cities in that province in order to keep it, because in truth there is no sure method of holding them except by despoiling them. And whoever becomes the ruler of a free city and does not destroy it, can expect to be destroyed by it, for it can always find a motive for rebellion in the name of liberty and of its ancient customs." He flipped back several pages and read, "It must be noted, that people must either be caressed or else annihilated; they will revenge themselves for small injuries, but cannot do so for great ones."

"Okay," I said, "how does Machiavelli recommend a small force should take control of a principality?"

"Hmmm," said Johnny, "let's see. Well, here he says, 'It cannot be called virtue to kill one's fellow-citizens, betray one's friends, be without faith, without pity, and without religion; by these methods one may indeed gain power, but not glory.'"

"I don't think that's it," Drew said.

"Give me that," said Victor, and took the book out of Johnny's hands. Johnny looked surprised, but said nothing, just got a distant, intent, fixed look on his face, and twisted his hands.

"Well Machiavelli says here that the best way to control a province is to establish colonies of your own people there to assert your influence over the locals for you," Victor said.

"Yeah, that's a great idea!" I said.

"Of course, you're supposed to start those colonies after you already took over," said Johnny doubtfully.

"Yeah, but in this case, wouldn't it make the takeover easier if we had some insiders ahead of time?" I persisted.

But while it was a fantastic idea, somehow we never got around to establishing a colony.

Still reading Machiavelli, Victor skipped to another bookmark and read aloud a passage that had been highlighted: "Where a citizen becomes ruler not through crime or intolerable violence, but by the favor of his fellow-citizens, this may be called a civic principality. To attain this position depends not entirely on worth or entirely on fortune. One attains it by help of popular favor, or by the favor of the aristocracy. For in every city these two opposite parties are to be found, arising from the desire of the populace to avoid the oppression of the great, and the desire of the great to command and oppress the people."

"Whoah," I said.

"But the problem with that," said Drew, without looking up from a different book which he was scanning for relevant quotes, "is that we have already agreed that it's not practical for any of us to win an election."

"Un-electable," Victor confirmed.

"Absolutely," Johnny agreed.

"So, then, is violence the only way to launch an invasion?" I asked, sounding somewhat pathetic as I said it, even to myself.

"Dude, I think that's a tautology," said Drew.

"I don't think the Roman Empire was established through peaceful negotiations," said Johnny.

At last Drew found the passage he had been searching for. "Friedrich Nietzsche," he said, and read us a long, disturbing passage:

"Here there is one thing we shall be the last to deny: he who knows certain 'good men' only as enemies knows only evil enemies, and the same men who are held so sternly in check among equals by custom, respect, usage, gratitude, and even more by mutual suspicion and jealousy, and who on the other hand in their relations with one another show themselves so resourceful in consideration, self-control, delicacy, loyalty, pride, and friendship—once they go outside, where the strange, the stranger is found, they are not much better than uncaged beasts of prey. There they savor a freedom from all social constraints, they compensate themselves in the wilderness for the tension engendered by protracted confinement and enclosure within the peace of society, they go back to the innocent conscience of the beast of prey, as triumphant monsters who perhaps emerge from a ghastly procession of murder, arson, rape, and torture, exhilarated and undisturbed of soul, as if it were no more than a students' prank, convinced they have provided the poets with a lot more material for song and praise. One cannot fail to see at the bottom of all these noble races the beast of prey, the splendid blond beast prowling about avidly in search of spoil and victory; this hidden core needs to erupt from time to time, the animal has to get out again and go back to the wilderness: the Roman, Arabian, Germanic, Japanese nobility, the Homeric heroes, the Scandinavian Vikings— they all shared this need."

"Hey," I said, "that's kind of like this, from *Crime and Punishment*." And I too read aloud:

"I maintain that all legislators and leaders of men, such as Lycurgus, Solon, Mahomet, Napoleon, and so on, were all without exception criminals, from the very fact that, making a new law, they transgressed the ancient one, handed down from their ancestors and held sacred by the people, and they did not stop short at bloodshed either, if that bloodshed—often of innocent persons fighting bravely in defense of ancient law —were of use to their cause. It's remarkable in fact, that the majority, indeed, of these benefactors and leaders of humanity were guilty of terrible carnage. In short, I maintain that all great men or even men a little out of the common... must from their very nature be criminals. Otherwise it's hard for them to get out of the common rut; and to remain in the common rut is what they can't submit to, from their very nature again, and to my mind they ought not, indeed, to submit to it. You see that there is nothing particularly new in all that. The same thing has been printed and read a thousand times before."

"Wow," agreed Victor. "To Nietzsche, great men are beasts of prey; to Dostoevsky, great men are criminals. I can see a similarity in their arguments."

"All right," said Johnny, "all this literary masturbation is fabulous, but the point is that only by taking out the police station can we prevent a coordinated response from law enforcement when we hit the other targets. The police station is where they coordinate all the police cars. They have all the communications equipment, the personnel, the resources; so if you want to take control of an area, then you have to first take control away from those who would otherwise have the power to stop you."

Eventually, with supreme reluctance, through the words of some of history's greatest thinkers, I allowed myself to be persuaded that there was no way to accomplish our goal without killing anyone; for, to paraphrase the immortal words of the renowned political philosopher Niccolò Machiavelli,

"Sometimes a great man must do things which are not good; for sometimes doing such things is necessary, in order for him to become or remain a prince."

Chapter 11

It turned out that Ramon's friend Lamont was able to tell us how to concoct a high impact explosive, and how to procure a large quantity of the necessary ingredients without attracting attention.

"It's not much of a fucking secret," said Lamont. "It's in the fucking dictionary. They describe it in the movie *Fight Club*. Mostly, you get a large quantity of some fatty substance, and you add a certain amount of an alkaline substance, such as lye. Lye is a highly concentrated potassium hydroxide, or sometimes sodium hydroxide," Lamont continued in exactly the same voice. "When you add it to a fatty substance, you create glycerol. Then," Lamont went on, "you add some nitric acid, which is derived from the oxidation of ammonia. And finally," Lamont concluded, "you add a dash of sulfuric acid, for good measure."

Lamont had a thoroughly formulated plan in mind, which he explained to us.

We would use olive oil as the fatty substance: hundreds of gallons of olive oil. We would get it from the same company that would sell us the lye, as well as the big tubs to mix it all in. We would tell them we wanted to start a natural soap company, and we would buy some essential oils and shit just to make it look legit. Johnny and Victor could even file for a business license with the State, to keep it all above board, in case anybody came around asking questions.

"Yeah," I said out loud, in one of those moments when I wish I had been quiet, "and we can set up a soap selling website, and we could all give soap away to our families for the holidays."

Nobody said anything for a moment, and then they continued the conversation without me.

"Dude," said Victor to the room in general and to Lamont particularly, "that is so fucking gay."

"What?" asked Lamont in surprise. "No, it—"

"G-A-Y, gay. I mean, here we are, planning all this terror and mayhem, and suddenly you want to start a fucking natural soap company? With organic fucking olive oil, no less. You have even picked out the essential oils already! Do you read Ladies Home Journal or something? Are you some kind of dirty hippie? What the fuck is this shit?"

Lamont was not amused, but kept remarkably calm. He stepped closer to Victor and observed coldly, "I'm talking about making a whole lot of nitroglycerin, motherfucker. I think that's pretty fucking serious."

Victor backed up a step but maintained his barking dog belligerence. "Fucking floral scented soap is for pussies."

Things might have gotten ugly, but Johnny interrupted and said, "Actually, you know, I think Lamont's got a really good idea."

Victor, who had been about to launch into a drunken, expletive-laced tirade, suddenly lapsed into a startled silence and stared at Johnny as though he had unexpectedly turned out to be a giant bug with waving tentacles.

"I like the idea of starting a front business," Johnny continued with his characteristic nonchalance. "Just think: we could take out a small business loan to finance our militia!" There was another pause, after which Johnny offered, "On reflection, maybe we don't want anyone looking that closely at our finances."

"Actually, nitroglycerin might be too unstable for our purposes," offered Drew. "What's our plan?" he continued. "We're going to mix up a huge batch of highly unstable liquid explosives, and then drive it in the back of a moving truck for hours out to our target? Or do you want to be mixing the shit on site during the operation? That sounds like a lot of trouble to me."

"Well," said Lamont, "once you've got the glycerin, you can use it to make dynamite, or—"

"Or what about gasoline?" interrupted Victor, who had opened a volume from the encyclopedia on the shelf. "Check this out: Pound for pound, gasoline has fifteen times the energy of TNT." He looked up. "So, we could start a different kind of front business," he continued as though we had encouraged him. "Like, a transport company. We buy a truck, and then it would be a legitimate reason to stockpile gasoline in drums, plus we could use the vehicle to transport troops and supplies during the operation."

"I thought we were going to use stolen vehicles during the operation," said Drew.

"One less we have to steal," suggested Victor.

"No way," I objected. "It would be too easily traced back to us. We can't use one of our own vehicles for the operation. That would totally blow our cover."

"I think you'd better get used to the idea that once this operation starts, our cover is blown," said Victor. "Either we win and succeed in holding the town permanently; or else we fail, and they will hunt us down like a pack of dogs. Therefore, we must win; and to do so, we need the best equipment and supplies available. I think we should start a trucking company and stockpile gasoline, which is a very powerful explosive."

"There's a problem with that," said Johnny. "Gasoline as a liquid burns; but only the vapor is explosive. Despite what you see in the movies, gasoline is not very good for blowing things up." He looked back at Lamont. "I like the dynamite idea though."

"Wait, here's a thought," said Drew, who was surfing Wikipedia on his mobile phone. "What about a fertilizer bomb? They've been used by insurgents in Iraq; plus that's essentially what those right-wing wackos used to blow up the Federal Building in Oklahoma City. You steal a truckload of ammonium nitrate fertilizer, and you can make the whole thing explode if you set it off with a charge, like a grenade, or dynamite, or whatever."

"If we stole a truckload of something explosive, then federal agents would start looking for us," I objected.

"Dude," suggested Victor, "don't you think they're probably looking for us already?"

"Different agents," I said, holding my ground for once. "The ones looking into potential domestic terrorism have a lot more resources at their disposal than the ones investigating a local bank job."

"All right then," said Ramon, "how about this? You use a charge of dynamite, or some grenades or C4 or whatever, to set off a shitload of fertilizer and to simultaneously vaporize a couple fifty gallon drums of gasoline."

"That should just about do it," said Johnny admiringly.

"All right," said Ramon, "here's what we do." And he proceeded to set forth our plan.

We sent several different guys to several different gardening supply stores, and accumulated almost a ton of fertilizer, buying it a little bit at a time from each store, careful not to send any one guy back to the same store twice, always procuring some seeds and gloves or clippers or something at the same time, to avoid attracting attention; and always paying cash, to avoid detection.

Lamont then built the remote detonator himself, to the admiration of us all. He did not even work out of any kind of training manual or anything; he just soldered it all together from a garage door opener and some spare parts in only a few hours.

*   *   *

Soon we ran out of money, surprisingly soon considering how much money we had stolen.

But we had bought a lot of guns and drugs and female companionship; and money goes fast under those circumstances.

As for female companionship, mine said her name was Lydia. She was Mexican or maybe Filipino, I never asked. She looked 24, maybe 26 years old but how can say. She was totally hot, and that was all that mattered. She came over with one of the other girls one night, and she fit in so well she just kind of stayed. I got to know her a bit through mundane conversation while I was washing dishes; and I was flattered when she chose to sit next to me, one evening when everyone was hanging out in the living room. The first time we made love we were standing up, behind the house, kissing furiously, the edges of her dress tickling my legs, my trousers around my ankles, with our friends just around the corner; we hoped they were unaware but in that moment we were both too enamored to care. My relationship with her didn't last long but it didn't have to. For a few glorious weeks she was my lover and her perfect thighs entangled me all night and I spurted my warm semen over her taut sweaty belly with my face between her perfect perky breasts.

At about the time she began to tire of me, or maybe I began to tire of her and treated her in ways that made her respond as though she was tired of me, well who cares anyway, we grew tired of each other, and at about that time our group realized we were nearly out of money: dangerously low on funds. And that's when we called up our army and readied our store of munitions.

It was less of an army than we had hoped. Initially when we were looking at the numbers from a rational perspective, we determined that our objective would be to get together a thousand, five thousand, ten thousand foot soldiers – now that would be a formidable army! Several weeks later we held an emergency conference to discuss contingency plans for a force of fewer than 500, in the event we would be unable to reliably muster more than that.

In the end we brought together a hundred and twenty-three recruits, including ourselves, and Ramon and his gang; and we felt like we had done pretty well. Secretly recruiting for an illegal operation turned out to be hard work, and we didn't have cash to offer signing bonuses. Now that the time came, it was going to be impossible to militarily achieve our primary objective, which was to completely take over. Instead, we decided to execute our fallback plan, which was to go kick some ass.

Chapter 12

We loaded up at the farm the night before I-day.

We milled around in the field outside the old house, drinking and getting high: one hundred twenty-three men and women, all dressed in black, many with sunglasses, toting duffel bags and hiking backpacks that bulged oddly. Gathered together in our numbers at that moment, we represented a broad cross section of society: with all of our racial backgrounds, African, Asian, Latino, Mediterranean, and European; with all our personal styles, from hip hop gangster to hippie goth to cowboy to skate punk; and with all our various political affiliations.

Yes, we had a blue-haired battalion of white women all dressed in matching black T-shirts with rainbow lettering that read "Smash the Patriarchy." They were proclaiming that they were going to go shoot white men in the name of antiracism.

But on the other hand, we also had a division of Deplorables in matching black T-shirts screen printed with orange Q snake logos. They were proclaiming that they were going to go shoot unbelievers in the name of Christ.

Not me. Fuck politics. I was just going to go shoot people for the hell of it. That's war, baby!

We had compromised with the extremists in order to bolster our numbers. It made me feel dirty, but it was necessary, at least for now.

Our operation had managed, at least temporarily, to bring together people from all these diverse backgrounds and ideologies, all of us united by the ultimate goal of finally being important, and not being bored.

There were men wearing eyeliner and women with close-cropped hair; men with long hair and men with shaved heads; women with blue hair, blonde hair, brown hair, red hair, and cornrows; men sporting an assortment of beards, goatees and sideburns; women in combat boots, men in cowboy boots; and members of both sexes who sported tattoos and multiple piercings in unusual places. Every one of us was carrying backpacks and duffel bags stuffed full of weapons and gear. We were prepared to launch our assault.

We were the dispossessed claiming what was someone else's, claiming it as our own by right of conquest, which is the oldest and most widely recognized right: certainly a more well-understood right than the will of the people, which, after all, can be manipulated by a sly government, or by a foreign government's covert intelligence propaganda operation, or by an unethical corporate media, or by the sheer willful ignorance and stupidity of human beings. The right of conquest, by contrast, is a precursor even to the divine right of kings. Indeed, conquest is the foundation of kingship, for only once dominion has been established can the king claim to be favored by heaven.

So we too would claim to be chosen by God, if anyone asked, once we had the town under our control.

How obvious is this? Can anyone see us? I wondered, looking around.

It might have been obvious to any casual onlooker that we were planning something nefarious. We were doubtless a shady looking bunch, and we were not being quiet or even particularly secretive at this point. It was time to roll before we gave ourselves away.

During our planning, when we had tried to figure out how to transport everyone on our team to the target, Victor proposed that we should try to steal a bunch of cars and several "big rig" 18-wheel trucks from a rest area. "So we send one team to a rest area along the highway in a stolen bus," he said. "When they get there, they block the exit with the bus and pile out and swarm throughout the area, quickly, trying to overrun everyone there before they can react. They confiscate all wallets, purses, car keys and cell phones; then they destroy the pay phone and drive away in an army of stolen vehicles: pickups, big rigs, station wagons and minivans. They split up into squadrons, each of which approaches the target destination from a different direction, stopping along the way at predetermined locations to pick up carloads of waiting personnel."

"I don't know, man," I said, always cautious. "That might not be such a good idea. It would be better to only have to steal vehicles on arrival. If we pull a parking lot heist when we're hours away from our destination, then they will be looking for us, and we lose the element of surprise. It decreases our chances."

Eventually even I gave up all hope of remaining anonymous, and our army caravanned most of the way to the target in our members' own personal vehicles. We drove all night, intent on reaching our destination before dawn so we would have time to get into position without attracting attention. A few of us slept, but many of us were too excited. At a certain turnoff, our vehicles split up to approach the target town from different directions.

We had gone over maps, the target's local phone book, and satellite photos from the Internet. We even drove out to the town we intended to invade, Johnny and Victor and Drew and I went there one day, drove around, checked out the banks, had lunch at a local diner, and planned our operation.

We planned to attack from all sides in numerous small teams, hitting several objectives simultaneously. We synchronized watches so no other signal would be necessary.

There were no rousing inspirational speeches. Because we did not attack *en masse* as a group converging on a single point, there was no opportunity for Johnny to emulate his heroes from Tolkien by delivering an impassioned and blood-warming oration to the front line of a waiting army. It's just as well. Our army might have wandered away in boredom while he was speechifying.

At precisely 11 o'clock in the morning, vehicles on every single street into or out of town caused accidents that blocked the road. As civilian commuters pulled to a frightened stop behind the wrecks, masked gunmen poured out of the vehicles that had caused the accidents. The gunmen commandeered the cars of the terrified onlookers, and intentionally smashed those cars right into the other wrecked cars in the center of the road.

Leaving armed garrisons to man each of the barricades, the rest of the gunmen advanced on foot towards central downtown, sending the good citizens screaming in fear before their advance as they shot out the tires of cars driving down the street, evicted the occupants, doused the cars with gasoline and set them on fire.

Meanwhile, at precisely 11 o'clock in the morning, four banks and the town's two adjacent big box retail stores were robbed by teams of masked gunmen.

Johnny, Victor, Ramon and Lamont each led a team that hit one of the banks; but I got to lead the team that went on the "anarchist shopping spree." Sure, we took the cash from the registers, but frankly, most people only pay with a card anymore these days, and besides, at 11 in the morning all they had in the till was some petty cash to make change. No, the haul was in the goods, and we stocked up: canned food, boxed food, bottled water, beer, wine, soda, clothes for everyone, some jewelry to help the guys get laid; shopping carts full of electronics; a whole crate of prepaid cell phones; and an assortment of construction supplies: cement, lumber, nails, wire, lots of tools. We must have been quite a sight, a black-clothed, well-armed militia stocking up on essentials, including toilet paper. We loaded all the stolen goods into some stolen delivery trucks, and then our team drove to the rendezvous point.

Meanwhile, at 10:58 am, the most important of the primary objectives was initiated. It had been difficult for me to accept this aspect of our operation, as I have already related.

It was Drew who carried out this essential component of our plan. We provided him with a specially outfitted truck and said, "Drive to this address. The directions are printed on this card. Drive up on the curb, drive all the way up to the front door, then get out of the cab and run like hell. Once you're well away from the truck, press this button."

"Got it."

So many things could have gone wrong. For example, Drew might have been pulled over a block from his target, and that might have led the cops on a high speed chase that ended with a suicide truck bombing.

But that did not happen. He drove right up to the building, drove straight over the curb and plowed through some trellising. Officers came running out of the building to chase him as he ran away from his illegally parked vehicle.

I didn't set out to be a bad person. I was just bored with my predictable life, and I thought maybe taking over the world would be fun.

But in order to take control of an area, you have to disable its existing systems of command, control and communication. We didn't have nearly enough guys or equipment to try to simply storm a modern police station, even one in a small town well outside a major city. A police station, we decided, was more heavily defended than a government building; so we decided to storm the courthouse instead. The police station would have to be decommissioned in another manner.

It was a terrible crime to have partaken in the planning and execution of such a murderous attack. The retribution I received later was well deserved. I was a spot of blight on humanity, an unpardonable criminal.

I had resigned myself to all of that with a shrug. We were about to declare war, and there are casualties in any warfare. You can try to justify it by talking about omelets, or you can cut the bullshit and admit that killing people for power is the entire point of fighting a war.

I was robbing a retail store at the time, but I can imagine how the scene went down at the police station when Drew set off the car bomb.

Though he had known it would happen, Drew was unprepared for the magnitude of the explosion. It was so loud it shook the ground. Pieces of truck and concrete flew through the air past his head.

Immediately, bursts of automatic rifle fire rang out from all his fellow invaders standing around him, and startled him out of the shock he felt from the blast. Drew raised his own weapon but could see no point in firing it; all he could see was dust and smoke anyway. He wondered if his comrades could even see him, or if they were about to hit him with a ricocheting bullet; and at this thought he screamed, "Hold your fire!"

It took a few more bursts for our side to cut it out; they were pretty keyed up by this point. Drew found it interesting that he had taken the initiative to issue a command, and that the troops with him had raggedly obeyed it. Johnny and Ramon were generally considered our group's leaders; most people thought of Drew as just one of their friends. But his order had seemed appropriate, nay, imperative. Sensing that he was channeling the moment, Drew decided to go with the flow.

"Let's wait for the dust to clear," he called out. "Then we're going to rush the building and shoot anything that moves. Where's that megaphone?"

It was found and handed to him. He pointed it at the station. "Is that clear?" he shouted through the megaphone, his voice amplified and distorted. "If you don't want us to fucking kill you, lie down on the fucking floor. If you lie down and don't move, and surrender your weapons, we will not harm you and we will allow medical personnel to care for the wounded. If you move, you will die."

In response a shot rang out and struck the tree behind which he was standing. Several positions in our line returned fire, and, considering this was the best cover he was likely to expect, Drew led the charge into the ruined station with a huge throaty bellowing scream like a raging mad half-bull demon, his scream amplified through the megaphone and transformed into some evil, mind-melting mechanical sound of triumph and disaster.

Drew tossed aside the megaphone. There was no need to use the front door: the bomb had removed most of the front of the building. The team lobbed a few canisters of tear gas through every opening they could see and donned their goggles and gas masks.

The team met with some resistance and took a few casualties but they were greater in number and better armed than the personnel inside the station's front area, and they had the element of surprise.

The police station had secure interior "pods" towards the back where the holding cells were, but this was no prison break; the attackers didn't bother trying to get in there, they just posted a few guys outside the door to make sure nobody came out.

After a few minutes of intensive firefight, everyone in the station was lying down. The invaders handcuffed and disarmed the survivors.

They were too late to have prevented the dispatch operator from calling the sheriff or more likely the new Homeland Security hotline. In our planning, we had sincerely hoped that the bomb might disable the communications equipment, but upon entering the room it appeared operational. Drew and the other gunmen cleared the room, doused it with gasoline, shot the communications equipment full of holes and set it on fire.

Drew and his team disarmed all the officers, even the dead. They locked up those who weren't critically injured and placed the entire station area under guard. Then they stormed through town in stolen police cars, snarling traffic and wreaking destruction all the way to City Hall.

City Hall was the final destination. We had strategically stationed a number of teams to maintain the town's perimeter, and left a team to guard our prisoners at what was left of the police station, but everyone else, once they had accomplished their primary objectives, converged on City Hall. Several of the bank teams were pursued to the rendezvous point by police cars, but the standoff did not last long; the few mobile police units were unprepared for our numbers and our munitions. Some of the officers were killed in the line of duty, and the rest surrendered and were disarmed, handcuffed, and locked up.

We massed our forces and stormed City Hall, which also housed the Courthouse. We were in luck. The City Council was meeting with the Mayor, and court was in session too. We took the Mayor and the City Council hostage; also the BIPoC judge, the District Attorney in her expensive suit, and some harried and overworked balding public defender, as well as about two dozen clerks and support staff. There were a few police and security officers throughout the building, but when they saw how many of us there were, they put down their weapons and we handcuffed them and put them out of the way.

Then we unloaded our gear into the building and began the fortification process. We blocked off most of the outside doors and windows, for starters. We built concrete barricades and blast walls. We turned City Hall into a fortress.

After that, it was time to celebrate. We had accomplished our ultimate dream. The National Guard had not yet arrived, and we actually controlled the town. It was ours! We were the rulers.

Now that the inconceivable had come to pass and we were still alive, some of the troops started to have second thoughts about following through with the next phase of our plan. As we enjoyed our newfound totalitarian power for most of a day and overnight, there was dissent. Someone said, "Shouldn't we just take the money and split?"

"Yeah," agreed another, "Let's just take the money and get the fuck out of here."

But the original four of us still held onto the dream of civic control, militarily enforced, and for a fleeting moment we thought we had attained our goal. Our plan seemed to have worked out and everything was going so well.

"Are you kidding me?" asked Johnny. "After all we've been through, at the culmination of our plans, when we're about to achieve, when we have *already* achieved so much, everything we ever dreamed of, and now you want to just chickenshit out? Well I have news for you, bucko: you wouldn't last twelve hours out there, not after this.

You think they don't know you were here, that your membership in the Hillsboro Militia has been kept secret? Guess again. They already have a file on you, with pictures and detailed biographical information, cross-referenced and collated, and summarized, and frequently updated. As soon as they heard about this little incident they ran a computer function keyed to an algorithm that told them definitively, beyond a shadow of a doubt that you were one of us. To confirm it, they checked and found that you were neither home nor at work today. Now they have bulletins out, wanted posters with your name and face, and if you go back out there they will be looking for you and they will pick you up within hours. The local police, the Sheriff, the State Police, the FBI, the CIA, the NSA, they will all have a fucking price on your head. You go back out there, and you're dead, or best-case scenario, a jailbird. Better to stay here and be one of the rulers of this, our domain." And he swept his hand majestically to indicate the utterly destroyed war zone we had created, and all the debris and detritus that littered the scene like the volcanic aftermath of a war god's tantrum, favorite toys hurtled to and fro and broken and smoking.

But then everything fell apart and went horribly wrong.

Chapter 13

Early in the morning at our headquarters in City Hall, a call came in over the radio from one of the barricades. Our guys there had been kept busy all night telling locals that they were not allowed to enter or leave town until further notice. This being small town America, it wasn't long before some of those locals went home and got their guns; and then our barricades were useless because we were being fired upon from within the perimeter. The barricade team reported that they didn't know how long they would be able to hold their position while surrounded by a numerically superior group of redneck freedom fighters carrying shotguns and hunting rifles.

I left City Hall with a small group of recruits. We drove a police cruiser out to the barricade with sirens blazing.

Then we used the vehicle to run down the vigilante locals, who only realized too late that the "police" were no longer on their side. The vanguard of the vigilante group didn't even have time to turn their guns on us before the grille on the front of the cruiser crushed them to the concrete.

The rest of the group scattered. While someone else drove, I leaned out the window and shot those fleeing patriots in the back. When we couldn't see any more who could still walk, we got out of the squad car and executed the wounded with point-blank head shots. A few of them I opened their jugulars with my super-sharpened kitchen knives to save ammo. So much for my claim to pacifism.

Blood-spattered and nerve wracked, we were just finishing this gruesome project when we heard a loud rumbling engine and a high-pitched whirring.

"Helicopter!" I screamed, and lifted my automatic rifle to the sky just in time to see a military helicopter rise up from behind a row of trees and houses.

The door gunner began firing at us at the same time I began firing at them. They had much larger caliber ammunition, but there were many more of us. We must have hit the pilot, because the helicopter lurched and a few moments later it went down and erupted in a giant fireball.

I radioed back to the other group that the authorities had definitely been notified. I got a reply, but it was garbled, I could not make it out.

I was about to head back to our City Hall front when we heard a new rumbling noise approaching. *What will it be?* I wondered. *Large-wheeled troop carriers, or actual tanks?*

It was an armored truck with a high-caliber machine gun mounted on the roof. *There's just one truck*, I noticed, and I didn't know if I should be elated or frightened. *What could the implications be? Did the other trucks go to the other barricades? Were there other helicopters?*

That was all the time I had for wondering; and then the gunner on the armored personnel carrier was spraying the barricade with artillery fire.

One of our team managed to get off a clear shot with a shoulder fired rocket launcher that took off the front wheel of the vehicle. The driver tried to keep driving, but the vehicle was disabled. Meanwhile the gunner on the vehicle's roof kept shooting at us. He very nearly got the woman who had fired the RPG.

"Hey!" I screamed at those Army soldiers through the din. "Beat a hasty retreat and we'll let you go! Get the fuck out of here!"

I don't know if they heard me or not, but they kept firing at us, so eventually we had no choice but to take them out.

When the shooting stopped, the perimeter team had taken several casualties. I decided to stay on with them and maintain the perimeter with the surviving members.

We took control of the armored vehicle, and laboriously rearranged the barricade so its mounted machine gun could become a cornerstone of our defenses when the next wave arrived.

I regretted that we had been forced to completely disable the drive system on the vehicle, but it was the price we had to pay; we would not have been able to capture it otherwise. Still, that one big mounted gun was a valuable asset. With a gunner manning that artillery piece and two other militants firing smaller arms, we defended that barricade until the entire truck was completely blown up. I don't know what hit it; could have been a tank round, a mortar, or even a missile fired from the air. All I knew is that one moment one of our guys was up there and the next moment he was engulfed in a fireball.

After that, I didn't think we could hold the barricade any longer. The two remaining recruits and I got back into the police cruiser and slalomed through the tangled wrecks that blocked the streets all the way back to City Hall. We ditched the squad car, ran up the courthouse steps and arrived at the door just as two armored troop carriers were rounding the far corner on the other side.

Our companions had already sealed off the entrance.

"Hey! Let us in! Johnny! Ramon! Let us in!" we were all screaming.

Knife in hand, I was afraid that a nervous unprofessional guard inside the building would shoot us just for being there. It was a risk. I could see the muzzle of a gun, pointed at us from within.

But then the barricade was opened and the door cracked far enough for me to squeeze through. A bunch of our insurrectionists were there, crowded into the entranceway, and they looked scared. The recruit behind me came in through the barricade; and the guy behind her, walking backwards, started shooting at the troop carriers as they were pulling up in front of the building. They returned fire, and hit him in the shoulder. He wasn't wearing a Kevlar vest, and the bullet shattered his scapula and splattered blood all over the wall behind him. He fell backward through the barricade screaming, and we dragged him in and managed to get it closed before any more rounds made it inside.

I spotted Victor, talking in the corner with some of the guys from Ramon's group. "Hey, Victor," I said.

"There you are," he said. "What happened?"

"Oh, we shot down a helicopter and captured an artillery piece mounted on an armored personnel carrier, but then it got totally blown the fuck up, and we had to beat a hasty retreat."

"Dude, it sounds like you fought valiantly," he said. "Here, have a hit of this."

As I did, he ran through the sitrep.

"It turns out the team manning the barricade on the south end of town was completely crushed," Victor informed me, "and now the sheriff and the National Guard and the Army and the FBI or whatever, they've sent in an entire battalion after us. We've barricaded all the doors and most of the windows here, we have a team on the roof, and everybody near the main entrance is supplied with gas masks. We have the mayor, the entire city council, a judge, and a whole lot of staff all under guard in a courtroom upstairs. It's a high-value hostage situation. We feel confident that they won't try to break down the door under these circumstances."

"But once the building is surrounded, how will we get out?" I asked.

"Yeah, we're working on that."

We spread throughout the building and took up defensive positions. We had snipers in various offices overlooking the street on all sides of the building; we had a well-armed team on the roof; we had a team reinforcing the barricaded doors on the ground floor; and a couple of recruits were busily packing up our haul so we could make a quick escape when the time came.

I took up a position near a window in a corner office on the second floor, thankful that the building was made of sturdy brick. Peeping from behind a curtain, I risked a glance at our adversary, in order to estimate our chances.

It looked like the entire United States Army was parked across the street.

I put my automatic rifle down on a desk next to the window and started trashing the office, just because it was there.

I could hear someone shouting through a megaphone. It was difficult to tell, from this distance, what was being shouted, but it was something like, "Drop your weapons, release the hostages and get down on the ground." Apparently the army did not know how many of us there were, or how well armed we were.

Someone on our side shouted something at the troops, and their megaphone voice resumed, the words muffled but sounding menacing.

"You may not leave the premises," buzzed the megaphone again. "You are all under arrest. Drop your weapons and stand down immediately."

"Take them out," Johnny's voice crackled over my radio, startling me. "Take them all out."

From my position I did not have a clear shot at any troops, so I took aim with my machine gun and shot out the window of the Humvee nearest me. This was meant to scare them off, and to apprise them that they had underestimated us. But a few bullets from my machine gun, and from all the other machine guns pointed out of all the other windows by all the other militants spread throughout the building: all those bullets combined were not nearly so fearsome as the explosions caused by three or four rocket propelled grenades fired from the rooftop. The RPG's were still a lot less impressive than what you see in Hollywood movies, but it was a bigger light show than anything you see on a daily basis in the real world. One of the troop carriers went up in flames. It wasn't blown to pieces; it did not look like it had been hit by a small thermonuclear device; it just went up in flames. It was very nearly anticlimactic.

People were shouting. Their words were mushy; my ears were ringing from all the gunfire, but after far too long I worked out what they were saying. "Gas! Gas!" was the word being shouted up and down hallways as well as over the radio.

I was tired, slow to comprehend and slower to react. Gas reminded me of something. Was it gasoline? And incidentally, what was the fog filling the room, was it smoke from firing my gun indoors? Eventually it dawned on me that if I didn't find my gas mask immediately I was about to be incapacitated for real; not just stoned or stupid but actually on the floor writhing in convulsions.   It was around here somewhere. Where the fuck was it? In my rage when I had trashed the room, I had managed to bury my provisions under a pile of useless crap: city government paperwork and a broken piece of shit fax machine named "Beep." I threw things around in a panic.

Finally I found my gas mask and managed to cover my eyes and mouth, a little too late. Some of the tear gas had gotten me. My eyes were streaming and I could not see. Those fuckers. I wanted revenge for this newest injury.

I pulled the pin from a grenade and tossed it out the window. It didn't even matter if I hit them; I just wanted them to know that I was not down. They got the message all right; almost instantaneously the window in my office was blasted into a million fragments by incoming gunfire from positions up and down their line.

Covered in shards of broken glass, I hunkered down on the floor, hoping none of the ricocheting bullets would lodge in my skull.

Then the shooting stopped, and I heard shouting.

I could not hear well, but after several minutes I understood that our hostages were on display. Johnny and Ramon explained to the National Guard that if the firing continued, we would start executing hostages, beginning with clerks and secretaries, and working our way up to the City Council and finally the judge and the Mayor. They were trying to negotiate our safe passage out of the building, but the negotiator for the military was having none of it. He kept insisting that our only option was surrender. Finally I took careful aim and shot him, but the next negotiator was no better. It occurred to me that they were just stalling for time, but I could not figure out what they were waiting for.

Then the world went up in flames.

An Air Force F-18 dropped a precision-guided one-ton bomb on City Hall and blew us all to little smithereens.

A militia can start a war; but only an army can finish a war.

In the media, the government spokespeople would blame us for the deaths of the Mayor and the City Council and the judge and the lawyers and everyone else. America's military leaders would never publicly admit that they had made a conscious decision to go ahead and kill the hostages along with all the rest of us just so they could end the standoff.

And although the propaganda was based on a lie of omission, even so it's true that I was, in my own way, responsible for the deaths of all those civilians, police officers, and government officials; as well as the deaths of one hundred twenty-two of my fellow violent insurrectionists, plus myself.

I spent my final moments looking at my own bowels, which had spilled out onto the broken concrete in a pool of my gushing blood. As I lay there, dying in unspeakable agonizing pain, I knew that this was more or less what I had expected all along.

Nonetheless, I was filled with a sense of victory. I had achieved my objective: I had transformed myself from just some guy into a legendary figure.

Yes, even in defeat I was now a great man, like Robert E. Lee, or Napoleon Bonaparte, or Alexander the Great. I was not born a great man; but I killed a bunch of innocent people, and I stole a lot of money, and with a little help from my friends I completely destroyed an entire town. Having done these things, I now felt myself to be the equal of any other great historical figure: great warriors such as Genghis Khan, Ramses II, and Julius Caesar; great leaders like Joseph Stalin, Mao Zedong, and George W. Bush.

Perhaps someday there will be a museum dedicated to me, subversive college coursework about my life, and down-home patriotic songs twanging on country music radio stations pondering how much better life might be for us all, if only I had won the Battle of Hillsboro.

THE END

THE END